S0-BAO-336

Amazon River Vets

Romance straight out of the rain forest…

Sisters and vets Maria and Celine Dias's beloved animal sanctuary is in jeopardy. Their brother ran off with the wife of their biggest donor, and now their funding has been pulled! If they can't find financial support, then the charity that's been in their family for generations will have to close its doors.

The clinic has also been an emotional sanctuary for the sisters. When they've been at their lowest, it's been the one constant in both of their lives other than each other. But will it still be there now that they are about to experience the biggest highs of their lives?

Read Maria and Rafael's story in
The Vet's Convenient Bride

Discover Celine and Darius's story in
The Secret She Kept from Dr. Delgado

Both available now!

Dear Reader,

Thank you so much for picking up *The Vet's Convenient Bride* and giving it a shot. This book is the first one in the Amazon River Vets duet— a series that has been a labor of love for me.

If you are new to me, you'll find that a lot of my books take place in South America or Brazil, because I'm from Brazil and I'm grateful that I once more get to tell the story of strong and passionate medical professionals who share the same background as I do. I'm especially excited to introduce you to the Dias sisters, Maria and Celine, who both aspire to make the world a better place through what they do with their animal charity.

In this book, you will meet Maria and Rafael, who have found their way into each other's lives through the animal rescue charity Maria runs. When the charity is on the verge of shutting down, Rafael offers to help her out with a donation. As it turns out, she is the only one able to help him access the funds through marriage.

I hope you enjoy their journey as much as I enjoyed writing it!

Luana <3

THE VET'S
CONVENIENT BRIDE

———

LUANA DaROSA

HARLEQUIN
MEDICAL
ROMANCE

If you purchased this book without a cover you should be aware
that this book is stolen property. It was reported as "unsold and
destroyed" to the publisher, and neither the author nor the
publisher has received any payment for this "stripped book."

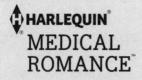

HARLEQUIN®
MEDICAL
ROMANCE™

Recycling programs
for this product may
not exist in your area.

ISBN-13: 978-1-335-59494-5

The Vet's Convenient Bride

Copyright © 2023 by Luana DaRosa

All rights reserved. No part of this book may be used or reproduced in
any manner whatsoever without written permission except in the case of
brief quotations embodied in critical articles and reviews.

This is a work of fiction. Names, characters, places and incidents
are either the product of the author's imagination or are used fictitiously.
Any resemblance to actual persons, living or dead, businesses,
companies, events or locales is entirely coincidental.

For questions and comments about the quality of this book,
please contact us at CustomerService@Harlequin.com.

Harlequin Enterprises ULC
22 Adelaide St. West, 41st Floor
Toronto, Ontario M5H 4E3, Canada
www.Harlequin.com

Printed in U.S.A.

Once at home in sunny Brazil, **Luana DaRosa** has since lived on three different continents, though her favorite romantic location remains the tropical places of Latin America. When she's not typing away at her latest romance novel or reading about love, Luana is either crocheting, buying yarn she doesn't need or chasing her bunnies around her house. She lives with her partner in a cozy town in the south of England. Find her on Twitter under the handle @ludarosabooks.

Books by Luana DaRosa

Harlequin Medical Romance

Falling for Her Off-Limits Boss
Her Secret Rio Baby
Falling Again for the Brazilian Doc

Visit the Author Profile page at Harlequin.com.

For Kery from Durban North Vets, who is the real-life Maria and adopts any homeless animal that comes her way.

Praise for
Luana DaRosa

"I think this was a really solid debut and I'm very excited to see what we get next from Luana DaRosa! She did a wonderful job executing and capturing the internal conflicts and struggles of both Emma and Dr. Henderson! It was a beautiful journey to go on with these characters."

—*Goodreads* on *Falling for Her Off-Limits Boss*

CHAPTER ONE

A LONG SIGH that spoke of the myriad sleepless nights Maria had struggled through over the last weeks dropped from her lips. Exhaustion sat deep in her bones, and there was no end in sight.

'Looking at the accounts again?'

Maria looked up from her desk and received the cup of coffee her sister Celine held out with a grateful smile.

'*Obrigada*, this was exactly what I needed,' she whispered into the brew as she basked in its aroma streaming up her nose.

'So, what's up?'

Maria took a long sip, avoiding her sister's piercing gaze for a moment as her face vanished behind the coffee mug. 'It's…not looking too good, Celine,' she finally said with a frown she saw reflected on her sister's face.

'Daniel really screwed us over,' Celine mumbled, and drew a scoff from Maria's throat.

'That's putting it mildly.' She would have used much more vulgar language to describe her deadbeat brother. Without his poor decision-making and downright betrayal of the family, she wouldn't struggle to pay the bills so they could keep the doors of their animal sanctuary open.

Their work already didn't pay well, even though their charity was a vital part of the community in Santarém. Nestled right along the Amazon River and surrounded by swathes of the rainforest, they provided services for the most vulnerable in their society—wild animals. They were the voiceless when it came to the deforestation works happening in the rainforest, so her grandparents had established this charity to help the animals in need. They might not be able to stop deforestation, but at least they could try and help the victims of these works.

They hadn't told anyone they were in financial trouble. The kind-hearted people of Santarém would probably sell their most expensive heirlooms just to keep the charity of Rodrigo and Alma Dias alive. Just as they had done when Gabriela, who ran the local charity shop, had fallen and broken her hip. Or when some vagrants broke into José's store and destroyed all of his machines. Both times the entire community had rallied around their members, giving whatever they could spare— and sometimes even more.

Maria's parents had continued their work because of that sense of belonging and togetherness. When they'd left to live out the rest of their retirement in Switzerland, the responsibility to continue had fallen to Maria, Celine and their brother, Daniel.

Because their animals had no owners and no one to claim them, they relied almost exclusively on donations from different sponsors. The lion's share of their monthly donations had come from a wealthy tech entrepreneur from Minas Gerais—that was until her brother ran off with the donor's wife.

The donations had stopped, and Maria had failed to attract new sponsors to make up what her brother had taken from them. They needed so much money to keep afloat, much more than anyone in Santarém could afford, that she didn't want to ask anyone. Because they wouldn't say no—they would just give. Only one option remained.

'We have to shut down,' Maria said into the quiet spreading between her and Celine. 'Even with the additional income from the vet clinic, we aren't even near to breaking even.'

In a last-ditch effort to keep her family's

legacy from shutting down for ever, Maria had hired an additional vet and started offering treatment for a wide range of domestic animals. She looked after any of the exotic and wild animals that needed rehabilitation, while Celine covered the farms in the area as a livestock veterinarian, and three months ago Dr Rafael Pedro had joined their clinic to look after the domestic pets of the area.

Regret constricted her chest when she thought of Rafael. He was a quiet man, not prone to sharing much of himself, yet they had still formed a friendship by co-existing in the same space—both in the practice and at home. Part of the deal for this job included the spare room in the Dias house.

Their areas of responsibility rarely overlapped. Despite that, something between them clicked into place as they worked around each other. A sense of connection, a live wire that crackled and sizzled with the heat and veiled longing.

Their conversations almost always turned flirty, leaving Maria with a sense of unfinished business. That there was something brewing between them was undeniable, yet an invisible boundary had stopped her from acting on the attraction. She was his boss, and though it had been a long time since she'd felt attracted to anyone like that, she couldn't go there with an employee. That would be inviting trouble into her own house. Literally. She didn't even know if he was interested or just being polite. The last time someone had asked her out had taken her by surprise.

Maurice, a *gringo* seeking investments in Brazil and owned of a company providing boat tours up and down parts of the Amazon River, had found an injured snake and instead of simply killing it he'd brought it to her so she could nurse it back to health and release it. After that, he'd come by a couple of times whenever he found something along the river, and eventually he'd asked her out on a date.

Though she had liked him enough, their relationship never went anywhere—her work always taking first place in her life. That much hadn't changed. If she wasn't here, she was at home taking care of her abandoned niece.

That didn't leave any room for romance, no matter what she sensed in the air between her and Rafael.

Celine seemed to have read her mind, for she smirked at her elder sister. 'Maybe if he's not our employee any more, you can finally ask him out.'

Maria rolled her eyes, but her pulse fell out

of step at her sister's words, sending her heart tumbling through her body.

She had to admit that Rafael caught her attention. Though the muscled arms and strong chest had drawn her immediate attention when he'd first arrived, it was the warmth in those hazel eyes that had her pulse racing. The way he spoke to distressed animals, handling them with such care as if they were his own family members, opened up something inside her that made her want to consider what Celine had just suggested. But when her brother left with his mistress, he didn't just doom their sanctuary. He also abandoned his daughter, to whom Maria was now a mother figure. She had a hard enough time understanding how Daniel could have done this to them—it got even harder when she tried explaining it to her niece.

'Maybe you should, since you seem so obsessed with him,' Maria deflected, and drew a laugh from her sister's lips.

'I'm legally still married, if you remember. Plus, I'm not the one making doe eyes at him every time I see him.'

'I'm telling you we have to shut our sanctuary down and all you can talk about is the hot vet I hired?' How had they landed on Rafael in the first place? There were so many more important things happening right now.

'Hah, so you *do* think he's hot.'

'Celine! Do you understand what I'm trying to tell you?'

'Of course I do.' Celine sighed. 'But I don't know what you want me to say. I'm devastated to close this place, but we both know you and I have done everything we can to stave off the inevitable.'

Maria sighed as the weariness in her chest grew heavier. 'I'll talk to Rafael first before calling the lawyer. He should know he's about to lose his job.'

Celine walked over to her, giving her a comforting pat on the shoulder. 'Let me know once you've spoken to the lawyer and what our next steps are.'

Maria nodded and when her sister closed the door behind her she let her head fall back onto the top of her office chair. She closed her eyes for a moment, willing her racing heart to slow down.

She needed to admit defeat and focus on rebuilding her niece's life, no matter if that put her own life's plans on hold—again. Her search for love, for a person to start a family with, hardly mattered when Mirabel had had the rug pulled out from under her by the one person who had sworn to protect her. She had ignored the longing clawing inside her chest for a long time, wanting to focus on her career first. She had thought there would be a moment where everything came together... or was she living that moment right now but unaware of it because she had never really *let* herself get attached to anyone?

Maria shouldn't even be thinking about this. Especially as she hadn't even asked the target of her attraction if he felt the same way and wanted to go out some time. But if they shut down the charity portion of the sanctuary, the vet clinic was all that remained. And, as much as she wanted him around, she didn't need another vet and she certainly couldn't afford it.

Maria would have to fire Rafael today.

Sweet and gorgeous Rafael. The innocent smiles and stolen glances they exchanged throughout the day sent jolts of unreserved happiness through a life marred with hardship. His friendship had become something she treasured, their passion for animals leading to an instant bond. Giving up on him was adding salt to her already mounting wounds.

If only things were different. That was the dream world Maria liked to escape to in the quiet moments, where her traitorous brother and empty bank account couldn't reach her, only the soft kisses of her would-be lover.

Not that Rafael had ever expressed such a desire for her, but the looks and the smiles were there, along with the gentle familiarity that came only from a friend.

Maria sighed again, leaning forward and burying her face in her hands. Maybe this was for the best. With the impending closure of the charity she had poured her heart and soul into, and becoming the full-time legal guardian of her niece, she had enough going on without needing to add romantic adventures to the mix.

Still, this conversation was going to suck.

Rafael sat behind the counter of the reception typing out his notes when the door to the clinic opened. 'Sorry, we are not open any more,' he said without looking up from the screen in front of him. But the soft shuffling of bare feet on the tiled floor only got louder.

Exhaustion sat deep in Rafael's bones, and he couldn't take on another walk-in. It was already after nine and he'd been woken up by a call from Emanuel, the owner of the local café, at an ungodly hour. The family dog, Rex, had sneaked into the pantry and found some chocolate he wasn't supposed to eat. At least

Emanuel knew his regular coffee order by now and had asked his son to deliver it, along with some pastries, as a thank you.

Because of that he had missed dinner with Maria and the Dias sisters' children. Even though he was a tenant and not a family member, Maria had invited him to dinner consistently until it became a habit. Those easy meals they spent together talking about their days in the clinic were a highlight of his days here in Santarém—along with the Sunday markets in the town square that they visited together.

He hated missing any of those occasions to speak to her, but he didn't get to decide when his patients would need him.

Paulo, the ten-year-old son of Irina, who ran the small grocery store in town, held a cardboard box out in front of him and looked somewhat lost. Rafael got off his seat with a furrowed brow. 'Paulo, what's the matter?' he asked as he circled around the reception desk separating them.

'My *mãe* told me to bring this here. She said you look after lost animals,' the boy said, and pushed the box into Rafael's hands.

He took it, placing it on the reception counter, and hissed when he opened the flaps to look inside. A kitten lay among some grass the boy and his mother had collected to make it feel more comfortable. Someone had ripped parts of its fur out from the neck and Rafael saw a deep cut further down. The blood had already congealed, closing the wound, but there was no way of telling if they had hit any vital organs.

'Where did you find it?' he asked, his eyes narrowing on the boy. It wouldn't be the first time he had to treat an animal that fell victim to the cruel whims of humans.

The boy seemed to sense Rafael's apprehension, for he lifted his hands in a gesture proclaiming innocence. 'We found it near the river and my *mãe* asked me to run here so you could take care of it. It was lying on the floor next to a small fire, but there wasn't anyone around when we got there.'

Rafael looked at him for a moment, considering his words. He knew that neither Paulo nor Irina would have hurt a kitten like that. They had their own clowder of cats running around town. Milo, the only black cat out of the bunch, regularly went to the river exploring, and came back with lots of trinkets and baubles. He must have led them there.

He nodded, closed the box again and lifted it off the counter. 'This kitten might have a shot thanks to you,' he said with a small smile and a wave as the boy left, before vanishing into the exam room, where he took the injured animal out of the cardboard box and lay it on the table.

'Okay, let's have a look at you.' He stepped closer, his hands gentle as he began his exam. He stopped in his tracks when he noticed the markings on the remaining fur, his brow furrowing. 'You're not a domestic cat...'

Rafael placed his hand under the animal, propping it up as he looked at its face, prising the lips open to examine its teeth. 'Are you a baby ocelot?'

With the size of the kitten, it was hard to tell, but the markings on its fur were not ones commonly found in domestic cats, especially not in a rural region like this one where most people kept barn cats.

The ocelot didn't even flinch when he probed at the stab wound. 'You've been hanging in there for quite some time, haven't you?' he mumbled as he picked his patient up and took its temperature, careful to keep it tucked in under his arm to reduce the stress on the already suffering animal.

'Forty point three... Higher than we would like it to be, but that might be from the stress more than anything else.' Rafael set the ocelot down again and frowned. Big cats like ocelots were part of the overall training they received, but he hadn't worked with them since veterinary school. He was pretty sure he knew what to do—ultrasound to check for any internal bleeding and, if everything checked out, bandage the wound and set her to rest.

Were the topical anaesthetics the same as for domestic cats? Doubt crept into his mind and Rafael sighed. He needed to check in with Maria. He glanced at the clock, frowning. Interrupting her this late wasn't something he wanted to do, even though he knew she'd want to know about the ocelot in their care.

Ever since Rafael had started working at the clinic, the gorgeous owner of the charity had invaded every quiet moment afforded to him. Whenever his mind wandered, he'd inevitably think about her, wondering where she was or what she was doing. Missing her when he'd gone a day without seeing her.

A thought that was as ridiculous as they came. How was he so attached to her already, when all they did was talk about animal welfare? Or was it that kind of simplicity that drew him to her?

Because Maria was unlike any of the women who had entered his life. Granted, all of them were fame-hungry socialites who wanted to benefit from the wealth a romantic link to him promised. Through gossip papers and social media they all knew that the person who married Rafael Pedro would finally unlock the trust fund his famous grandparents had set up for him years ago.

One had almost succeeded in tricking him into marriage, setting up everything so perfectly that Rafael hadn't suspected anything until he stumbled upon the truth by accident. That was the moment he had disavowed his family and love altogether, instead dedicating his life to his work as a veterinary surgeon.

And Maria was his *friend*, one he cherished way more than he had originally planned— along with the entire village of Santarém. What had only ever been meant as an escape had become as close to home as he had ever felt. A large part of the credit went to Maria, who had taken the time to befriend him and introduce him to everyone in the village.

He could acknowledge all of that, yet the yearning within him grew louder, hotter, as they spent more time together. Whatever that was blooming in his chest, he needed to stomp it out right now—before it got out of hand.

Rafael picked up the ocelot again, placing her in a little pen next door to keep her comfortable while he stepped away. The main building was solely dedicated to the sanctuary's rehabilitation efforts. Outside of two small treatment rooms, there was also a bigger surgery and several rooms to house crates with their overnight and long-term patients. Next to this building was a smaller house where the Dias family—and he—lived.

Rafael breathed a sigh of relief when he saw the lights in the kitchen were still on. He opened the door, closing it silently behind him so as not to wake the children, and stepped into the kitchen to find Maria sitting at the table, her delicate fingers wrapped around a steaming mug of tea.

Her look of utter defeat as she glanced up at him stopped him dead in his tracks and, for a moment, he forgot why he was here as a bout of irrational protectiveness surged in his chest.

'What happened?' he asked before he could rethink it.

The shock on her face told him she hadn't realised he knew her well enough to read her expressions. She shook her head. 'Nothing,' she said, somewhat too quickly.

Rafael narrowed his eyes but decided not to pry. There were more pressing things happening in this moment.

'Hey, I need you for a quick consult,' he said, pushing all the unwelcome feelings and reactions towards Maria away.

'What's the matter?' The look of defeat vanished, replaced by concern as she got up from the chair.

'Someone dropped off an ocelot with a strange knife wound. Not sure what that's even about, but I just wanted to double-check my steps since I'm not sure how much wild cats deviate from the treatment of a house cat.'

Maria nodded and walked past him, motioning him to follow as they crossed the yard to get to the clinic. 'Did they rip out the fur of the ocelot too?'

Rafael nodded. 'It's alert but tired. I was going to suggest an ultrasound before we stitch it up.'

He led Maria through the door and she went onto her knees in front of the pen with the ocelot, stroking its exposed chest. 'Some people in the area ritually kill baby ocelots or monkeys. We occasionally get some of the failed sacrifices here to patch them back up.'

'What? The indigenous communities wouldn't do that, would they?'

Maria shook her head. 'They know the value of an animal's life much better than most of us do. No, it's a strange occult sect terrorising the local animals.'

Rafael swore under his breath, struggling to imagine how anyone could do such a thing. To think this happened often enough that Maria could recognise the injury on sight alone.

'It's breathing okay. Going by the angle, I don't think they hit any of her organs, but her temperature is elevated.'

'Could just be the stress,' Maria mused as she looked at the wound. 'Grab me the ultrasound.'

Rafael went to the storage room and grabbed the handheld device, dabbing some gel on the ocelot's chest before Maria placed the transducer on the skin, scrutinising the image on the screen.

'Doesn't look like there are any internal injuries,' Rafael said.

'The blade just missed this artery here.' She pointed at the screen and Rafael took note as she explained the surrounding organs.

'Should we stitch up the wound?' That was the part he'd been uncertain about and why he'd gone to look for Maria's advice. He wouldn't have suggested stitches on such a wound on a cat or small dog, but there were potentially other factors with wild cats he didn't know about.

Maria grabbed a sponge and gave the wound a careful wipe. 'No, this wound is a couple of hours' old at this point. We would do more harm than good if we disturb it. Best to observe and intervene if we find any infection.'

She picked up the ocelot and hugged it close to her chest for a moment, cooing as she petted its head. 'You poor thing. We'll get you back out there once you are all healed up.'

Rafael smiled at that small gesture, appreciating the place of compassion it came from. His profession was full of people with incredible drive and passion, yet in the three months since he'd been here, Maria had surpassed all expectations with her level of care for anyone coming through her door—animals and humans alike.

What a shame his parents had schemed and pushed so much that he'd lost any confidence in having a normal relationship with a woman without fearing for both his and her sanity. But after losing the one woman he'd ever loved to his family's plots, trust didn't come easy to him any more. Laura—his ex—had been in league with his parents all along, whispering sweet nothings into his ears and making him believe that he could find love after all. The brutal sting of rejection rose in his chest at the memory, reinforcing his ironclad defences.

Defences that didn't seem fortified enough. Watching Maria work and provide value to her community had such a profound impact on Rafael and the way he worked that he had caught himself fantasising about having this—her—for the rest of his life, as more than just the friend she was to him now.

The part of him that had been hurt in the past cautioned him to be careful, and it mingled with the fear of losing what he had built for himself here. Was it worth risking the friendship they shared for a shot at something more when he wasn't sure if he was broken beyond repair?

Maria felt the warmth of his stare on the back of her neck, sending a shiver down her spine. She stayed in the adjacent room for a moment and fought to find the strength within her to start the conversation she needed to have with Rafael. It didn't help that he'd stayed longer to help an injured ocelot that had found its way into their clinic—same as it didn't help how much she enjoyed seeing him every day, how much their friendship meant to her.

She bit her lip as she got back to her feet. This was beyond ridiculous. In the three months he'd been here, he'd not made a single move that would signal he wanted more. No, quite the opposite. Whenever they spoke, the sense between them was one of easy familiarity. There was no reason why this sort of heat should lick across her skin from a mere glance.

Taking a deep breath, she stood up straight and walked back into the room. An awkward silence spread between them as they shot each other tentative glances. How did one even start such a conversation?

She swallowed hard before she opened her mouth. 'Listen, while I have you…'

Rafael turned towards her, his hip leaning against the exam table as he looked at her with those hazel eyes that turned her insides into gooey puddles. Oh, God, why had she let the flirting go so far? Now her tongue suddenly felt too large for her mouth, unable to form the words she needed to say.

'The charity isn't doing so well at the moment. It hasn't been in a while if I'm honest.' She took a breath, her lips trembling when genuine concern lit up his eyes.

'Is that what's been bothering you this last week or so?' he asked.

Maria's eyes widened at that question, thinking back to the few moments they had shared since she'd woken up nine days ago and admitted to herself that the charity had to close. Of course he would have noticed.

She closed her eyes, focusing on the task in front of her as her mind drifted and heat rose in her body as she sensed the connection of genuine attraction zing to life between them once more. That was the last thing she needed to concern herself with.

Though when she opened them again Rafael's face was so full of concern for her that the heat pooling in the pit of her stomach exploded, sending sparks all around her body.

'Last year we lost our biggest sponsor. Ever since then we've been struggling to keep our heads above water. Opening the vet clinic was a last effort to see if the revenue would help us make ends meet.' Maria bit down on her lower lip, glad that her voice didn't crack as she delivered this news that she'd been dreading.

Rafael looked down at his feet as he crossed his arms, a sigh expanding his chest. 'Is there anything I can do to help?'

Maria's hand went to her chest as her pulse accelerated. Though she knew already there was nothing he could do, the fact that he'd bothered to ask opened something inside her that she wanted to remain closed. Now that they'd started this conversation, he'd be leaving soon, and along with him the sense of excitement and attraction that she hadn't felt in such a long time.

This small gift she'd received after all of the

turmoil she'd been through would fade away as well.

'No, unfortunately not. Unless you know someone who has some money they're looking to give away,' she said with a half-smile.

An expression flitted over his face, a strange sharpness entering his eyes that she couldn't understand. She watched as he took a few breaths, wanting to know the thoughts she could see building in the way he looked at her.

'I actually do know someone like that who would be willing to be your new benefactor.'

The warmth drained out of her body, replaced by an unearthly cold as she processed his words, hoping against hope that they were true and she wasn't just imagining them because those were the words she'd wanted to hear. A new benefactor? Someone to replace what Daniel had stolen from them with his reckless libido?

'What...? Who?' It didn't matter that she wouldn't recognise the name. If he knew someone who could keep the doors of their sanctuary open, she didn't care if it came with strings attached.

'Me,' Rafael said, and heat swept through her once more, colliding with the chill in her bones and whipping up her insides into a merciless storm.

'You? But…you live in my guest room.'

'Ah, yes. Unfortunately, my money is tied up in some clerical red tape.' He looked away, a flash of discomfort and self-doubt in his eyes. 'My grandparents set up a trust for me, but they wanted their hard-earned money to benefit me and my siblings only once we were ready to start our own families.'

Maria furrowed her brow, her eyes narrowing as she looked at him. Who were his grandparents that they'd left him so much money? 'Clerical red tape?'

Rafael chuckled, a sound that stoked the already brewing storm in the pit of her stomach. 'My grandparents thought the best way to ensure all the Pedro grandchildren used their money how they intended was to put in a clause which only allowed us to access the money once we were married.'

Her heart leapt inside her chest, crushing against her ribcage. Her eyes darted to his left hand, scanning for a ring but finding nothing but an empty finger. If he wasn't married, how was he going to become their new benefactor?

The thought of Rafael getting married caused a strange dissonance in her mind, and she shook her head to get rid of the fleeting sensation.

'I imagine you're not married since you're

telling me all of this.' The surge of hope she'd felt just a moment ago faded as quickly as it had appeared.

'No, I'm not married.' He paused for a moment, and the sudden intensity in his eyes made her breath catch in her throat.

Maria could hear nothing but her own heartbeat thundering through her ears as she realised what Rafael had just suggested. That couldn't be real. Was he seriously suggesting that *they* should get married? No, such a thing didn't happen in real life. This was the plot of a *novela*.

'I'm not sure I follow,' she forced herself to say, her voice sounding distant. 'Because what I think you're saying makes no sense.'

'Maria,' he said, and took a step closer, 'I think the solution to your problem is to get married.'

CHAPTER TWO

As THE WORDS tumbled out of his mouth and into existence Rafael released the deep breath he had been holding. A sense of panic had gripped him when he'd realised what Maria was about to do. The charity was running out of money and if he wanted to keep his job, if he wanted to help his friend and remain near *her*, he needed to fix the problem.

But there was only one way he could fix it, and that involved marrying Maria, who he'd been quietly attracted to since he'd started working here. A move he wasn't sure would be a smart one, bearing in mind what was at stake. Knowing his family, they would come crawling out of the woodwork the moment they realised he was married and had access to the money—putting Maria and her entire family in the line of fire if he stuck around for too long. They had been trying for years to get their hands on his money and would stop at nothing to get it. If they had no problems paying a woman to pretend to fall in love with him, they would find some way to turn Maria against him—use his feelings for her to get what they wanted The thought stung, sowing doubt in his mind when he wanted to commit.

Wasn't that the best use for his money, even if it meant he needed to give up his place here? His fortune had cursed him his entire life, maybe this was the only way to lift the taint from it.

But such a suggestion was absurd. Could he even propose something like that to her? He knew her to be a good person, a friend—more than that in his dreams. Someone he could trust with such an absurd suggestion—even if she thought him ridiculous.

It was a leap of faith. The worst she could do was to say no.

'You can't be serious right now. We are not...' Maria said, breaking the charged silence between them.

'This would be out of necessity and nothing else. If I can submit a marriage licence to the bank, they will release the last block on it and the money will be mine—yours, if you want it.' He hesitated for a moment. Rafael knew she was in a vulnerable position and the last thing he wanted was to apply any pressure.

'This would only be temporary. A few weeks to sort out the trust and then we can file for divorce,' he added to reassure her when he caught her sceptical glance.

Maria took a step back, leaning her backside against the exam table, her arms crossed in front of her chest. A myriad thoughts and emotions rippled over her face, each one so fleeting that he wasn't sure what she was thinking. He wasn't really sure what he was thinking either.

Though this proposal was a snap decision born out of desperation, Rafael became more convinced as this moment went on. His sacrifice would be well worth it if it meant the sanctuary could stay open. Though he'd only been here for three months, the people of Santarém had almost immediately opened their arms, accepting him simply because they saw him as the restless soul he was—and offered him a home. Something he hadn't had for so many years.

Wasn't that what the money *should* be used for, even if it meant he had to leave? How could he stand by and watch Maria—and the entire village by extension—suffer such a loss when he had everything he needed to help? Everything but one thing…

'This is…' She stopped herself, scrubbing

her hands over her face. 'I can't believe I'm considering this.'

Her voice sounded incredulous—a sentiment he could understand very well. After all, proposing marriage to his gorgeous boss was a first for him too. Maybe this hadn't been the most delicate way he could have put it. But she had been about to make a final decision about her sanctuary when she hadn't known that there was another way to help her keep the doors open.

'I get if you need some time to think,' he said to defuse the tension. 'I just want you to know that I'm serious about this. Both about giving you the money for your sanctuary and there being no strings attached to this arrangement. Nothing will change.'

There was no need to tell her how much he'd resisted marrying the women his parents had arranged for him to meet—or that the one woman he'd thought he would marry had left such deep scars that he'd vowed to never get emotionally attached to anyone again. Not while the curse of this trust persisted. Once people realised how much he was worth, their perception of him changed.

He hoped against hope that this wouldn't be the case here.

'How fast would you be able to get the money?' she asked after a while, and the question made his heart squeeze with hope.

'Once I submit the marriage licence to the lawyers, it should be a matter of weeks.'

Maria looked down at her feet, giving Rafael a view of the soft curve of her neck, her brown skin looking lush and soft even in the harsh light of the exam room. He had to bite back the impulse to reach out and touch her, trail his fingers along the sensual curves he saw underneath the uniform scrubs they all wore for work. An impulse he had to fight more often than he was ready to admit over the last couple of weeks. Her graceful sensuality had sneaked up on him until one day he'd found his gaze lingering longer and longer when it didn't need to.

The scent of freshly fallen rain and earth drifted towards him, igniting the need inside him he'd been fighting for so long. The impulse to step closer, to slide his hands into her thick hair as he pulled her face closer to his to inspect her dark pink lips with his eyes—and then with his mouth, to make sure they were just as soft as the visual examination suggested. To watch those brown eyes widen with surprise and pleasure as he explored her…

His throat constricted. Had this been a sound idea or had he just offered something he shouldn't have?

The air around them grew thicker with each passing second of silence, and Maria struggled to reconcile Rafael's suggestion with her own reaction to it. The word *no* had formed in her mind almost immediately, but her lips had refused to speak it. Of course she would not marry him. The very thought was ridiculous. So why did it make her heart beat so fast?

The looks, the fleeting moments they got to work together, and the warm trickle of sensation he caused to stir under her skin—those were not supposed to be real. They were small indulgences she let herself enjoy, idle fantasies for a woman who was not available for more than that. Not when she'd found herself with an unexpected child and mounting financial troubles. His suggestion had given life to something that shouldn't have been more than a shadowy emotion dwelling in her chest, the longing inside her no more than a *what if* that she found refuge in when things got too hard.

Because a non-committal *what if* was the only thing she had space for in her life right now. Mirabel and the charity took so much of her time and passion, there was no room for anything else—especially not if it was Rafael-shaped. His mere presence in the room demanded so much of her, the air became hard to breathe until all she could think about was those full lips moving against hers.

And along with it all came a question she couldn't figure out.

'Why are you offering this? What's in it for you?' The question left her mouth sounding indelicate, making her cringe as the words filled the air between them. She didn't mean to accuse him of anything.

Rafael picked up on this as well, frowning slightly. 'I…'

He stopped, hesitating as he furrowed his brow. Was he thinking about what could be in it for him?

'You're my…friend, and I happen to have the solution to your problem. Of course I would offer it up,' he said after another moment of silence and shrugged. 'I'm asking something pretty big of you in return. Even if I don't benefit from it, I know it's a lot to ask.'

Maria nodded, her suspicion melting away under the concerned gaze Rafael shot her. The last man she had trusted with anything so personal had been her brother, and he had betrayed her on such a magnitude that she found it hard to trust anyone—even the man who had become her friend over the weeks he had been working here. Now soon to become more if she went through with this...

'How much are you expecting to get?' she asked with a slight hesitation. She wasn't sure if she wanted to know. The confidence with which he'd suggested this fake marriage to her made her believe the sum to be large.

Why was she even asking? It wasn't as if she was going to say yes. That was unthinkable. When she thought about her future husband, he was someone who she had a deep emotional connection with, someone to share her life—like her parents had. Though that person was nowhere in sight, and Maria worried that she had put off the search for him for too long. Something else always took precedence. Her studies, her job, leading the charity. Now looking after Mirabel...

Was this how it was supposed to happen for her? Convenience rather than true love?

Rafael smirked, a look of amusement to hide something underneath that dazzling smile of his. Embarrassment? 'My grandparents amassed quite some wealth during their careers. They gave a lot to their son—my father. But they also set up these trusts for their grandchildren.' He hesitated for a moment, those golden-brown eyes narrowing on her and sending an unexpected shiver down her spine that shook her all the way to her core. 'I'm expecting around seventy-five million *real*.'

The room went dead quiet, to the point where Maria could hear the animals rustling in their pens next door. Her mouth was dry, unable to comprehend such a large number in her head. 'Seventy-five million *real*?' she repeated, just to make sure her brain hadn't invented a number. With that amount of money, she'd never have to worry about any donations ever again. Was that why he had suggested getting married? Because he wanted to gain access to the money himself? Maria still wasn't sure she understood his motivation.

Why not find someone to marry for real? He had everything any woman would swoon over. The short hair just long enough to dig your fingers through it, an athletic build to melt against, and the most trusting eyes she'd seen in a long time. It was those dark looks he shot her whenever they met in the clinic or at home that made her shudder in secret.

He could find someone to care for, to love. Why go through the trouble of getting a fake wife when he could find a real one in a matter of weeks?

As she looked at him her eyes wandered over to the clock hanging in the exam room, and she pushed herself straight. 'Come, let's sit down at the table. Such a discussion warrants another cup of tea.' She also needed to be back at the house in case one of the children needed her.

The kitchen and living area were empty when she ushered Rafael in—save for her Great Dane, who didn't even raise his head before he went back to sleep. Maria busied her hands at the counter, putting on the kettle and preparing two cups of Earl Grey as her head still spun from all the information he'd given her. When she sat across from him, a steaming mug in front of each of them, she finally found the resolve to look at him again. Seeing him sit at her kitchen table had become so normal, their conversation casual and light as they drank their coffee together or when they were having dinner with Celine and the kids.

Too normal, really. Having these moments with Rafael was something she cherished. Would it all go away if they got fake married?

'Who were your grandparents that they had such a fortune?' That piece of information had been bugging her since he'd revealed how big his inheritance was. She tried to think of any famous Pedros she had heard of, but too many came to mind. How could she narrow it down?

Were they vets too? Or was he the only one in his family?

'They invested in a production company that produced some popular *novelas*,' he said, sounding shorter than usual, and Maria bit her lip so as not to pry further. His grandparents had locked his inheritance behind getting married. Maybe their relationship had been complicated. If she knew anything, it was how draining complicated family relationships could be.

'How would this work? We just sign a paper and that's good enough? How do you imagine…us working?' The thought that there was an *us* type of situation was so strange Maria's heart squeezed inside her chest.

Rafael looked down at his tea, his fingers fiddling with the label of the tea bag in a rather uncharacteristic show of nerves. At work, he exuded an aura of confidence that only increased her struggle with her resolve not to steal another glance at him. The thought of being married to this man caused a multitude of opposing emotions to bloom in the pit of her stomach, making it hard to focus her thoughts on the moment.

This still wouldn't be real—if she actually went ahead with it. Even if they signed a paper, that didn't make them married. Just like Celine, whose husband had run out on her. They'd never signed the divorce papers, but that didn't mean her sister was married any more. Marriage required more than a signature on a piece of paper. Commitment, care… love. Those were the foundations of a marriage rooted in a mutual partnership. Without those things, their *marriage* would be just a piece of paper.

'I hadn't thought this far ahead. Up until the moment when I proposed this idea to you, I didn't realise this was what I was leaning towards.' He took a sip of his tea. 'When you spoke about your financial trouble, I wanted to help you. Being a part of Santarém's community has become important to me.'

There was something else as well. Maria could sense his hesitation, an unwillingness to put all of his cards on the table. Was this about his family again? There was clearly some tension, but he'd never spoken about his family or where he was from. This information hadn't mattered when Maria hired him. They still didn't matter since they would only be married on paper, but she wanted to know more anyway.

'We can go to Manaus, talk to my lawyer. I'm sure we can draft an agreement on what the conditions of this…marriage are to be. If we are both happy with it, we can go to the courthouse and sign the marriage licence.'

Maria searched his face as he spoke, looking for something, though she wasn't sure what that something was. Anything to raise a red flag, some kind of hint to tell her not to do this—because she was *so* close to doing this. This was the unexpected solution she had been praying for ever since Daniel left them.

But as she considered his proposal—in the most literal sense—Maria realised she would do a lot more to save her sanctuary. There were so many things she could imagine going wrong if she married the man she'd been flirting with for the last three months. The main one being that if she went ahead with this scheme, she would close the door for ever on any of the attraction becoming real. Money would exchange hands and that would alter whatever they had. It might even alter their easygoing friendship.

'Okay, if we're going to do this, we'll need to treat it like a business agreement and nothing else. I don't want either of us catching any feelings because we are pretend married and forced to act like that sometimes.' She paused, looking up from her mug as she acknowledged something neither of them had in the last few months. 'No more flirting with each other. That will only make things more complicated.'

There. Those were her terms. A part of her was certain she was making a big mistake, that two people couldn't just get married as part of a business deal. It just seemed to contradict everything she had believed about marriage growing up.

Except this wasn't a marriage. For all intents and purposes, this *was* a business deal. And she would do anything to keep her family's legacy alive, to keep helping the most vulnerable animals in their society when they depended on her for safety and care. Her own mother had sacrificed so much for this place; she couldn't let her brother be the end of that. Becoming a place of sanctuary for animals had become her life's work, her calling to it greater than anything else. The thought of giving up on it had robbed her of sleep, of her confidence and purpose. She couldn't let go of what brought her so much joy, what she had dedicated her life to. Especially not when there was a solution right at hand. No matter how strangely that opportunity had come into her life.

A fleeting look of surprise rippled over Rafael's face. Had he believed she would decline him?

* * *

Rafael didn't realise he'd been holding his breath. He let it loose, exhaling the full capacity of his lungs into the warm evening air. She'd said yes. The answer Rafael had been hoping for, despite his own trepidation.

There was no doubt in his mind that his family would get wind of this arrangement sooner or later. Their need for his money was far too great for them to just let him live his life. From the moment their media company had started to lose money, they had suggested he become an investor—brandishing their status as family like a weapon. They wanted to achieve the same level of fame that his grandparents had climbed to, and he'd learned in many painful lessons that nothing would stop them from trying. Not when that need had driven them to trick him into falling for one of their chosen candidates—breaking his trust in genuine love for ever.

What made him question his decision was the soft scent of subdued rain and earth drifting into his nose as he sat there watching Maria decide. It was a scent he wanted to get used to, one he yearned to smell in his bedroom as he drifted off to sleep—standing in direct opposition to the words she had just put out in the open. The fact that they had been dancing around each other for months without either of them making a move—their friendship the only thing they were brave enough to acknowledge.

Now, he needed to forget about the tantalising scent this woman left in her wake, testing his resolve ever since he'd taken up this position and moved into her house as part of his work assignment. This arrangement would not work if he let his attraction get the better of him.

'These seem like reasonable terms,' he said. 'And no more flirting.'

'So, what do we do next?' Maria stared down at her mug again, her wavy hair half obscuring her face and only adding to the almost irresistible mystery that was this woman.

'I'll call my lawyer in the morning to set everything up. I will let you know what documents he needs from you. Once we have an appointment at the courthouse we should take a trip to Manaus.' As he created their to-do list, he looked at her again, gauging her comfort level. He'd just dumped a lot of information on her, things he wasn't even sure about himself.

The agreement was more for Maria's benefit. He didn't need a piece of paper to hold him accountable for the things he had promised her, and he knew without question that she wouldn't abuse their faux marriage. Someone like Maria could never do that. Her integrity shone through every single action she took, something he admired about her. But he understood if she needed some sort of document to prove his intentions were just as pure.

Maria took her phone out of her pocket, swiping her finger over the display for a couple of moments. 'What about next Friday? Celine can cover the clinic that day. I'll just tell her we're both needed on a case in Manaus, so she'll watch the kids.'

Friday? That was a week from now. Rafael knew they were working on a tight deadline, but he hadn't expected it to be so soon. What had he expected? He wasn't sure, only that Friday felt close all of a sudden.

'I will check with my lawyer if we can get an appointment next Friday. Just…' He hesitated. 'Take some time to think it over.'

Maria nodded as she got to her feet, pushing the chair away. 'I'll check in on the ocelot tomorrow.'

'Thanks.' He smiled and his heart stuttered when her lips curved upwards in reciprocation, bringing a light to her face that was as breathtaking as she was. Their eyes lingered on each other for a second and he fought the urge to reach out, yearning to feel that kind smile under his fingers.

Why were these feelings emerging now, when they had more at stake than before? Or had his simmering feelings for her led him to make this preposterous proposition to begin with?

CHAPTER THREE

THEY WERE REALLY going to do this. Through some connections at city hall, Rafael's lawyer had managed to get them an appointment in a week's time. Had it only been seven days since they'd concocted this plan? Maria's heart pounded against her sternum, driving nervous energy through her body as she sat in the leather chair of this opulent office.

A part of her still wondered whether this was a good idea—a question she didn't have an answer for. Technically no—marrying the guy she had been attracted to since he'd stepped over the threshold of her animal sanctuary was a spectacularly bad idea. Marriage was such an intimate act, one she wanted to experience for real the way her parents and grandparents had. Had she waited too long, prioritised her career and passion over finding the right person to start her family with?

Maria had always thought she had plenty of

time to find herself as the leader of the charity and then she'd be able to think about love. But struggle after struggle had forced her to put it off.

Now she'd found herself in a situation where a fake marriage was looming in front of her, once again stopping her from going for what she really wanted—something real. But—and that was the part that won every internal argument she had with herself—she didn't have any other choice. The money Rafael promised her would keep the sanctuary running for a few years at least, buying her enough time to find another donor. Looking at the paper the lawyer handed her, she realised how much money they were talking about.

'You'll donate this?' Maria's voice was no more than a whisper as she looked down at the paper again. This was so much more than her signature could ever be worth.

Ever since their hour on the plane together, Maria's senses hummed with awareness of the man next to her and the reason why she had insisted on no flirting drifted further from her mind. Why had she said that when those moments together were the only ones she looked forward to during her day?

'This is all already promised to your charity once the bank releases the funds. And I believe you find the rest of the terms acceptable?' No doubt amused by her shock, he smiled and paused. He must have grown up wealthy too, seeing the inherent ease with which he navigated their current situation. Maria felt the sweat on her palms as she looked at the paper again, while he seemed calm and collected.

The agreement stipulated that neither of them would seek any kind of marital asset division or alimony once they signed the divorce papers. Maria didn't need a paper to hold herself to that. If this wasn't a genuine marriage, she would want nothing that belonged to Rafael.

'How long will…this last? You said it wouldn't take more than weeks for the bank to release the funds.' She realised she didn't even know how long she should expect to be married to him.

'Bureaucracy can be slow. It can take up to six months for city hall to issue a marriage certificate. But they usually arrive within thirty days,' the young lawyer, Sebastião, said to her.

Maria sent Rafael a questioning look. She knew there were a lot of things he wasn't telling her—like his underlying motivation. He said it was to help her—that he couldn't watch his friend struggle. But was that really all there was? Had her brother's betrayal shaken her confidence in the good intentions of people for ever, or was her hunch correct that Rafael had his own motives?

'Before you leave, I need you to know that I had my assistant change the hotel booking you requested from her to one room only,' Sebastião said with a pointed look at Rafael.

Rafael's eyebrows shot up, mimicking her own surprise at the lawyer's words. A sudden and visceral heat cascaded through her body, singeing the ends of her already frayed nerves. They had to share a hotel room? Her eyes shot over to Rafael and the nervousness that thought caused to bubble up within her must have been written on her face, for he looked back at the lawyer.

'Is that necessary? It's only one night, and you booked the plane tickets as well. There is no way they know I'm here.' Maria's ears pricked up at the last sentence as she glimpsed some of the personal history that informed his decision to marry her. Who were *they*? His family? An ex-partner?

The lawyer shrugged, as if expecting this protest from his client. 'You're underestimating them, Rafa. They may be watching you closer than you think.'

Rafael went still for a moment, his body and

face unmoving. Only his eyes darkened with a dangerous glint that sent a shiver down her spine. Whoever these people were, they were not in good standing with Rafael and from the look in his eyes alone, she knew that she never wanted to be his enemy.

A strange sense of protectiveness came over her. What had these people done to him?

'All right,' Rafael said in a tired voice, and reached for a pen to sign their agreement. He passed the pen to Maria, who only noticed her hand shaking when she reached out to grab it. He must have noticed too, for he drew his hand back a little, a small line appearing between his brows.

'Maria, are you—?'

'I'm fine,' she said, and squared her shoulders.

For most of her adult life she'd run the animal shelter by herself, and when her brother ran away, abandoning his own child, she'd stepped up to take care of her as if she were her own. A little piece of paper would not defeat her. Not when that piece of paper promised everything she needed for a brighter future.

Everything except maybe one thing.

That was what the tiny voice in her head whispered as she took the pen and scrawled her signature onto the paper to seal the deal. The fantasy of Rafael that she'd been tempted to act on was now gone. Despite the hardships and the struggles of the last year, Maria still believed in love and wanted to find the person to complete her. She'd ignored her own dreams and desires over the years because the time had never seemed right. Kept ignoring them now as she entered into this fake arrangement…even though in the quietest of moments Rafael made her dream of more.

With a shake of her head, she pushed those thoughts away and gave the paper back to the lawyer. 'So, what's next?' she asked, clearing her throat of the last remnants of her unbidden Rafael fantasy.

'There is a car waiting for you to take you to the courthouse. One of my clerks secured an appointment for you, so they will process you immediately.' The lawyer stood up from his chair and reached over his desk to shake Rafael's hand before turning to her and extending his hand again. Maria took it and plastered her most convincing smile on her face.

One more paper and her sanctuary would be safe.

The atmosphere in the courthouse was a lot different from what Rafael had prepared himself for. Though he wasn't sure what he *had* expected. Couples of varying ages sat in the waiting area, some dressed up for the occasion, some more casual, as if they had decided that today was the perfect day to make this long-term commitment to the person they loved. One thing they all had in common was the air around them, the aura of quiet celebration and...love.

It sent a shiver down Rafael's spine as he looked around and absorbed the energy of the surrounding people. By contrast, he and Maria must come across as downright miserable. Once he'd found himself in their camp, had been excited to spend the rest of his life with the woman he'd fallen in love with—only to find out she'd been pretending to love him for his money.

No other moment in his life had ever been so painful, teaching him a lesson he would never forget. As long as a relationship would unlock the money in his trust, he had to assume that none of the feelings were genuine. Rafael couldn't allow himself to trust anyone. The only reason Maria was different was because they were friends. Friends who might send each other heated looks, but friends nonetheless. Throughout his time in Santarém she had never pretended to be anything else.

'Feels like we're not representing the mood here,' Maria whispered, picking up on the same observation he had.

Her words had a calming effect on him. At least they could both admit that this situation was…weird.

'You're only missing out for a brief period. I'm sure you'll get to see that side of a wedding when this is all over,' he said, and hoped the smile on his face looked more genuine than it felt. There was something strange and upsetting about the thought of Maria with another man that raised the hair along his nape in defence. A flash of fury bloomed in his chest, one he shoved down and back into where it had sprung to life. She wasn't his, was never going to be either. No amount of rage would change that.

As soon as they presented themselves at the reception desk the court clerk waved them through to another room, passing more people waiting to sign their licences. Some couples had even brought a small contingent of their families to celebrate with them.

He pictured his family standing with him here today, and the smile on his lips died as quickly as it had appeared. Even if this were a genuine marriage, they would find some way to interfere. They would lie and deceive, turning his feelings for Maria against him until they got what they wanted. Or worse, they would somehow convince her that he was the problem.

That thought brought ice to his veins. The sooner he could give Maria the money and vanish again, the better.

Thirty days, the lawyer had advised him. Thirty days and then he'd be on his way again to find a place he might finally feel he belonged. He'd thought he'd found that place in Santarém. Working alongside Maria and Celine, getting to know the family and how they had been a part of the village for generations. Even though the close-knit community had seemed daunting, they'd accepted Rafael when they saw he genuinely wanted to belong. As if he were a stray in need of adoption.

The charity formed a strange but wonderful symbiosis with the rest of the village. Irina, the grocer, brought any food over that was about to spoil. Emanuel, who ran the café, brought them snacks whenever he saw the lights on late at night. They all worked together to make the dream of the Dias family come true, simply because they were one of them.

And Rafael had become one of them too, as he cared for their pets, treating their family members as if they were his own.

Not just the villagers, but Maria too had opened her home for him when he'd needed it. Though it was part of his working arrangement that she would provide him with a room, she also invited him to their family dinners each night. Or took him along on family outings to the weekly farmers' market or quiet walks along the river.

Rafael had never known he *wanted* to belong like that until it had happened.

It made leaving Santarém that much harder. But Sebastião was right. His family had set private investigators on him before, trying to unearth anything they could so they could force him back into the family fold and gain access to his funds. He'd have to stay under the radar until everything was done. Who knew what they would come up with if they learned he was finally married. He couldn't in good conscience bring this kind of energy into Maria's world when she had a daughter to protect—or rather a niece.

Rafael turned his gaze towards Maria as they followed the clerk down the corridor. He'd never asked about the circumstances that had led to her niece living with her. Could it have something to do with their financial problems as well? Did she have another sibling who'd passed away, leaving her to care for the child on her own?

The question burning on his lips died when they stopped in front of another desk.

'Dr Pedro and Dr Dias? Yes, I have you right here. Please follow my colleague. She will show you the room.' The receptionist waved her colleague over, handing her the envelope of forms the lawyer had given them with all the documents needed to get married.

She led them around the corner and through a door. A desk stood at the far end of the room, and several groups of chairs were arranged in neat lines. A couple sat in the very front row, surrounded by their friends who were chatting in quiet but animated voices.

'If you sit here at the back, the judge will get to you,' the woman said as she gave Rafael the envelope and left the room.

He glanced at the other couple once more before offering a chair to Maria and sitting down next to her. Her fingers were woven into each other and lay still in her lap. With a stiff spine, she looked straight ahead, her expression veiled and unreadable.

'Are you okay?' It wasn't the first time he'd asked that today, the need to check in with her a constant hum in his mind.

She nodded, her lips a thin line. 'Can I ask

you a question?' she said after a prolonged silence, her voice low and melodic, seeping through his skin and igniting a strange heat in his chest.

'Anything,' he said with a nod, and startled himself when he realised he meant it. Because from the way her eyes drifted down to her hands, he could already tell what this was going to be about.

'Who are you so afraid could find us that your lawyer had to book everything for us?' She looked back up, her brown eyes narrow, bracing for whatever uncomfortable answer she had come up with.

Rafael hesitated, taking a deep breath to calm the intensity her lingering gaze had created. Not the question he'd expected, yet so much more personal than he was ready to admit to her. But Rafael couldn't deny that she deserved the truth—at least a part of it. Despite his best efforts, he *was* putting her near the line of fire.

'Mostly my parents. They have been trying to get me to marry a partner of their choice for some time,' he said, selecting each word with care. 'They made some regrettable decisions about their business. Instead of calling it quits, they pressured my siblings and I to invest in their business. Since my siblings are chasing the same fame my grandparents had, they jumped at the opportunity—and lost all of their money as well.'

Maria's features softened, a spark of understanding lighting up her eyes. 'You ran as far away from them as you could. I was wondering what brought you to Santarém. Whenever new people arrive it's usually because of personal circumstances.'

Rafael nodded and waited for the usual apprehension to flood his system whenever he spoke about his parents. But none manifested. A sense of calm remained, urging him to continue speaking.

'I knew if I stayed close to them they would eventually wear me down and get their say. Family is such an important thing—which makes escaping the grasps of a toxic one even harder.'

His heart squeezed tight when Maria nodded with a deep understanding that could only come from someone who had experienced something similar. The urge to reach out to her face and stroke the slight frown away thundered through him and he balled his hand into a fist to resist.

'Okay, who were your grandparents? Because when I heard the amount of money they had left you, I knew they must be famous. But there are so many famous Pedros, I wouldn't even know where to start.' Her lips curved up in a smile, as if she had been waiting for this detail.

That curiosity was what he needed. Even though he didn't enjoy talking about his famous grandparents, it was preferable to exposing how much he yearned to touch her in this moment.

'They were a pair of actors who made it big in different *novelas* in the sixties.' He paused for a moment, unable to stop a smirk from tugging at the corners of his lips. The next part sounded so unbelievable. 'They were best known for their roles when they played a very slow-burn romantic couple set in a…veterinary clinic.'

Maria's eyes widened and the blush blooming in her cheeks was exquisite. He had to ball his hand into a fist again to stop himself from reaching out to brush over her delicate skin.

'An actor and actress named Pedro…' she mumbled, seemingly to herself, and a second later her face lit up with recognition. 'Your grandparents were the couple in *Patas Para O Amor*?'

Rafael groaned. 'Please don't tell me you've watched that *novela*.'

'Are you kidding me? Celine and I used to watch it with our mother. She says the reason she went into veterinary medicine was because of that show. If it weren't for that, she would have never met my father.' Maria laughed, a sound so clear and full of genuine joy. His heart stuttered in his chest, making it hard to breathe for a moment.

'Didn't they end up bringing *Patas Para O Amor* to the US?' she asked, unaware of the heat she had caused to cascade through his body.

He nodded. 'That's where they made the fortune that my parents and siblings squandered away on their own attempts at fame.'

Maria lowered her eyes. 'Seems no one escapes complicated family drama,' she said, the smile fading away.

'You speak from experience?' His question must have touched something within her, for a hurt expression flitted over her face, showing him a wealth of pain before the walls around her came back up, leaving him on the outside—wondering.

The judge called their names and both of them stiffened, falling back into reality and remembering what they'd come here to do.

'You ready?' he asked, and Maria nodded.
'Let's go.'

* * *

The couple and their friends were still sitting in the front row, waiting their turn, when she and Rafael stepped up to the desk. Her heart slammed against her chest when he handed the envelope to the judge, who pulled out their documents to verify their identities and process their marriage licence.

'Are you with a party?' the judge asked, and Maria hesitated, looking at the man who was going to become her husband in the next few minutes.

'Ah…no,' he said, shaking his head. 'It's long overdue that we have our licence issued.'

And though Maria's heart was already working overtime, her pulse spiked when Rafael looked at her with a genuine smile on his lips as he took her hand and breathed a featherlight kiss onto her skin. Their connection created a spark, which sent a blast of heat from her arm down to her core.

This wasn't real, but rather another layer to their ruse to make their marriage look believable. His lawyer had warned them about any scrutiny they might face. For anyone outside of themselves, this marriage was supposed to look real.

So Maria did something dangerous—she stopped fighting the attraction rising between them. It would help her, she thought, to pretend they were an actual couple. Just for this day, until they were back at home and could go about their lives again.

She looked at him, her hand still close to his lips, and instead of fighting it she gave him the longing smile she had always wanted to.

The judge nodded, picked up her pen and signed the forms in front of her. She then picked up a hefty stamp, pressing it onto the open ink pad. With a slam that resonated in Maria's bones, she stamped the piece of paper.

Rafael released her hand and stepped forward when the judge turned the paper around for him to sign. She could feel the warmth of his body radiating towards her, fuelling her own heat. He placed the pen on the paper with no hesitation, signing his name on the indicated line. Then he stepped back, holding his hand out to her.

Maria took the pen and focused on the paper in front of her. A small tremble shook her hand as she put the tip down on the line and she hesitated, the weight of what she was about to do coming down on her shoulders. This was the price she had to pay to keep her sanctuary from financial ruin.

She swallowed the lump in her throat and signed her name with a flutter in her stomach.

The pen came down on the table with a clang of finality. Done.

Maria was now married to Rafael.

They turned to look at each other, an unbidden current springing to life in her chest and arcing through the air between them. She shivered, biting her lower lip to stop her heart from racing and keeping her mind in the present. Nothing they were doing was real. It was all a ruse. The heat in her veins, the quiver in her stomach—they were the results of the circumstances and not true feelings.

Loud clapping jolted her out of the moment passing between them, and her head whipped around. The other party in the room cheered at them, clapping and hooting for the union they thought was as real as their own.

Maria's spine stiffened when someone from the group called out, 'Aren't you going to kiss your bride?'

Cheers erupted again, and Rafael glanced at her with a slight frown. The question in his eyes was easy to read. He wanted to know if he could kiss her.

That wasn't how she'd imagined their first kiss would go. In her fantasy there had been a lot more courting and genuine romance, not this subterfuge to keep up appearances since his family's eyes and ears could be everywhere.

Maria swallowed and gave the faintest of nods. His features softened at her consent and everything around her slowed down as his hands wrapped around hers, pulling her closer to him. His scent enveloped her, the smell of lavender and something primal which eluded words. A tremble shuddered through her when she watched his hazel eyes narrow and his face come closer.

For a moment, Maria couldn't breathe as anticipation thickened the air. Then his lips brushed against hers, and the connection this touch created stoked the tiny flame she'd been carrying for Rafael into a roaring fire that pumped through her veins with every beat of her racing heart.

His hands kept her steady. She could barely hear the cheers from the group behind them, with the blood rushing through her ears, her pulse hammering against the base of her throat.

And as her lips moved against his—as the onslaught of desire consumed her—Rafael broke their connection. He took a step back to look at her, but his hands remained in place around hers. The ghost of a smile tugged at his mouth, and the look he gave her melted her insides.

They both jumped when the judge next to them slammed her stamp again onto the form they'd just signed before signing it and handing it back to them. Rafael let go of her hands, and that withdrawal was enough to plunge her back into reality.

'There you go,' the judge said as Rafael received the paper. 'You are now husband and wife. Your licence will be mailed to you in the next few weeks.'

This isn't real.

Maria repeated the mantra in her head as the heat from his kiss receded. Yet no matter how often she spoke those words in her mind, the memory of the fire licking in his eyes seared itself into her brain, almost wiping out every other thought about him. Was this just her imagination conjuring things that weren't there—or had Rafael lingered on her lips before he'd broken it off?

'Let's go.' His soft-spoken prompt ripped her out of her thoughts, and she looked at him. He'd taken her hand again and was now tugging her along as they left the building and entered the car already waiting for them. The car which would take them to the hotel they'd be staying at—sharing one room.

Maria swallowed again.

This wasn't real, no matter what she felt when Rafael touched her.

CHAPTER FOUR

THE PHANTOM OF the all too brief kiss they'd shared burned on his lips for the entire twenty-minute car ride to the hotel at the edge of Manaus. They stayed quiet, the air around them growing so tense each breath became a struggle to keep steady.

This feeling—the heated desire he bridled with every ounce of his strength—was not part of the plan. His attraction to her had been undeniable from the moment he'd started working at her clinic, where they'd become close enough to consider each other friends. The closeness they shared at work, the nightly dinners, the weekends at the farmers' market—he'd let himself believe that, because of those, she thought the same way about him. That the stolen glances and secret smiles spoke of a desire to make more of their friendship, but he knew better than to let himself indulge in that idle fantasy. Because he knew that his family would do anything they could to get him to surrender his part of the inheritance—including going after his wife.

Her reaction to his kiss was a clear indicator that his attraction towards her wasn't reciprocated. Why else would she tense up like that, seconds after his lips had brushed over hers?

Had he already ruined this entire scheme with one action? It hadn't even been his idea, though his heart had picked up speed when the group of strangers had shouted their suggestion at them. Kissing those full lips had been an unfulfilled fantasy for several weeks now.

Though in those daydreams he had never kissed her because they had entered into a fake marriage. That was a development he hadn't seen coming. Soon the money would be his—hers—and he would have to give up the one place that had become home to him.

'What are you going to do once we get to the end of this arrangement?' Maria asked into the quiet, as if she had picked up on the direction his thoughts were heading.

'I…' He hesitated, his mind forming words that his lips struggled to say. He wasn't going to tell her that he planned on leaving. How could he? Rafael didn't want to acknowledge that fact himself, let alone put the words out into the universe. 'I haven't thought about it much. To be honest with you, I never thought I would get access to the money because I ruled out marriage as an option early on.'

Her brown eyes flicked towards him in an expression that caused emotion to thunder through him in a confusing force of attraction and apprehension.

'You never wanted to get married?' she asked him after a beat of silence.

Was that disappointment lacing her words? A thickness coated his voice when he answered. 'No, I knew early into adulthood that marriage would not be fulfilling for me.'

'Why is that?' she asked, the same timbre in her voice giving him pause, constraining his chest as his heart squeezed tight.

Why didn't he want to get married? Because the concept of it had been weaponised against him from the moment he was old enough to understand how his grandparents had set up his trust. That had also been the moment when his parents started to push every single girl in his direction who would make what they deemed a good match—the only criteria being her family history and how they could gain from it. And even though he knew what they were capable of, he'd never thought they could be so heartless as to conspire with a woman to get him to fall for her so they could share the payout.

He hadn't believed Laura to be capable of that either, which showed that people would say anything if the sum of money was large enough.

But this trauma sat so deep in his bones, had so irrevocably shaped him as the person he was now, he couldn't let it go. He had lived such a solitary life, trust didn't come easy to him.

'I didn't grow up with a very stable role model of marriage. Neither my parents nor my siblings had what I would call successful marriages. They were far too concerned with what they could do with my grandparents' fortune to focus on their relationships. That obsession and dependency became their primary motivation for being together, even though they were—and still are—making each other miserable.'

He paused as an all too familiar bitterness rose in his throat, giving the words that followed the bite of ancient hurt. 'They claim to love each other, but that clearly wasn't a good enough foundation to save them from their own greed. So I decided to give up on the thought of marriage, of love. I would rather be alone than put anyone through the agony I see mirrored in my family every day.'

Rafael paused, the words tumbling out of his mouth before he could reconsider how much he wanted to share with her. It almost sounded like a warning.

Do not dare to fall in love with me.

'What about your siblings? You said they took their cue from your parents?' Her voice was soft now, a small frown creasing her brow as she absorbed the information.

'They did. My brother and sister are a few years older, so their turn came earlier than mine. But they had already bought in to the notion of fame my parents were yearning for and were eager to do their part. I don't know how I turned out different from them…'

Rafael's stomach lurched when a delicate hand appeared in his field of vision, her long fingers brushing against the top of his hand that was curled into a fist. Sympathy brightened her face, making him inhale sharply at the sight.

'I'm glad you didn't. Family is so important in our culture, it's hard to distance yourself from it, even if you know that's the best for you,' she said, her hand hovering over his as if she were thinking about wrapping her fingers around it.

A thought that brought a thrill to his chest. An inappropriate thrill that he needed to subdue before it turned into a spark.

'Don't feel bad. Because of my parents' fame-hungry attitude I grew up with a nanny, whose family owned a farm where she would often take me. I think without her, I wouldn't have become a vet.' Hiring someone else to raise him had been the only sane thing his parents had ever done for him. Camila had begun working for the family when their old nanny retired. By that time his siblings were already too infatuated with the image of fame and money.

Not Rafael. At ten the concept didn't interest him much, so when Camila started to take him to the farm his parents didn't object—his teenage siblings were old enough to look after themselves.

'A farm? I would have thought that would lead to a career similar to Celine's rather than family pets,' Maria said with a quirk of her lips.

'It was an option. Though I really bonded with the barn cats, to the point where they would follow me around the grounds all day.' A fond memory he hadn't thought of in such a long time, and one he was glad to share. The topics they had previously been talking about might leave the impression there was nothing redeemable about him either. What if she thought he was no different than his family, marrying her out of necessity and not love? He couldn't let that happen…

'Don't worry about us, though. Our arrangement here is different, and it's because of you and your charity that I wanted to do this. If it can buy you some time to find a new long-term donor, I'll gladly deal with some discomfort.'

Her hand stilled at his words, and the moment he said them Rafael regretted his poor choice of word. Had he just suggested that being near her was causing him discomfort? It was, but in an abstract and affection-starved way that he couldn't possibly explain to her without making it sound as if he had ulterior motives in marrying her.

How could he explain that his own attraction to her was the reason for any discomfort?

'I mean—' he started, the car coming to a halt interrupting him.

Before he had a chance to elaborate the meaning of his words further, the driver got out and opened Maria's door for her. She looked back at him and the disappointment in her eyes cut a lot deeper than he'd thought was possible.

* * *

They walked over to reception, where Maria could see a member of staff already waiting for them, clearly expecting them. Rafael remained right beside her as he handled the entire interaction with very few words. Clearly the lawyer had impressed on the hotel staff that they were to treat these two with the utmost discretion as they arrived in their car with tinted windows.

These were the lengths he'd go to for his safety—and hers by extension. What awful things had his family done to him for him to request something like this?

Though they had been spending a lot of time together as friends, Rafael didn't share a lot about his past—which she could understand. Though she regularly complained about Celine, or shared her struggles around raising Mirabel, she stayed away from the topic that hurt the most. Daniel. Of course the same would go for Rafael sharing his past only to a certain extent.

Today, though, she sensed they had taken the next step. Maria's traitorous heart had squeezed so tight when he'd spoken about his family, about his shattered belief in love—that he never wanted to get married. How uncomfortable it was to even be fake married to her.

The last part had stung a lot more than she cared to admit. Because this wasn't real. She didn't want this to be real because she *did* believe in love. Once the dust had settled, Maria hoped she could focus on that rather than her abandoned niece or the demise of her animal sanctuary.

Not that she had much experience on how to go about her search. Her most recent relationship had ended last year, when Daniel disappeared. Though she had enjoyed spending time with Maurice, there had been a distinct lack of a spark that had given her pause.

She believed there was someone out there for her to make her family complete, and that when she met that person there would be no doubt, the way there had been with Maurice. No, that missing piece was still out there, just waiting for her to discover it.

Rafael Pedro was not it. No missing piece of hers could carry such a pessimistic belief about love and marriage within his heart and remain compatible with her. What worried her about that was the sinking feeling in the pit of her stomach at this very realisation.

Her thoughts were interrupted when the woman at reception handed Rafael their key cards and pointed at the elevator.

He approached her, his hand coming to rest

on the small of her back, where each finger left a searing indentation as they strode towards the elevator that would lead them to their room. Where they would share a bed.

The heat pooling below the skin of her back where his hand still lay exploded through her at that thought, settling in the pit of her stomach and streaking across her cheekbones.

Rafael stepped back when the elevator doors closed, pressing the button for their floor before giving her a tentative smile that only served to intensify the heat in her face.

'Don't worry about it. I can sleep on the floor,' he said into the silence.

Maria opened her mouth to reply when the elevator stopped and the doors slid open, admitting another person, who selected the eighth floor. Both fell silent, but she felt Rafael gravitate towards her while eyeing the stranger with a cool expression.

She remained quiet as they passed two more floors before they halted again, the six on the display lighting up as the doors opened to their floor.

Rafael ushered her out, his hand still firmly planted on her back, and as they stepped out he looked back, making eye contact with the person remaining in the elevator as the doors closed.

'You know them?' Maria asked, following his gaze.

'No, I don't think so. But we can never be too careful with my family,' he mumbled under his breath, as if he still expected the person inside the elevator to hear them and report back to the invisible phantom that was his family.

'What did they do to you?' she asked before she could think better of it.

Her brother, Daniel, had done unforgivable things, abandoned his daughter for the woman he had an affair with, yet even that pain didn't seem to compare with what he'd experienced with his family if that was his reaction to a stranger in an elevator.

Rafael didn't reply but walked with her to their designated room in silence, swiping the key card over the pad and letting them into the room where they'd be spending the night. Together.

Maria's brain went blank at that thought, her feet freezing before the threshold. Almost an hour had passed since they'd left the courthouse to come here, yet the moment she remembered what waited behind this door the memory of their kiss resurfaced. The warmth and softness of his lips had been intoxicating, even though the kiss had been no more than the gentlest of brushes. It raised the tiny hairs along her arms, a shiver trickling through her body that she tried, and failed, to suppress. The moment she realised how much she was enjoying the touch her body went rigid.

'You okay?' he asked when she didn't move.

'Um…yes,' she said, daring to take a step into the room.

Rafael went ahead, flicking on the light switch to illuminate the space. The cool blast of the air-con enveloped her as she stepped in, and she only noticed then the thickness of the humid heat surrounding them. It was a heat she was used to from living close to the Amazon and the rainforest. Though Manaus was a large city, it bordered on large parts of the rainforest, so much that they had seen several monkey troops in some side alleys as they'd driven to the hotel.

It was the cool air that drew her attention to the sweat on her skin, making her wonder if this was only from the heat or if Rafael had anything to do with it. It would be far better for her sanity if it was only the heat.

'Ah, this is perfect,' she heard Rafael say, and saw what he was referring to a moment later when she reached the end of the corridor that opened up into a spacious suite.

Rafael lay sprawled on a couch on the far

side of the room, his arms tucked under his head and looking at her with a satisfied smile. 'I can take the couch.'

Maria barely heard the words he spoke over the thundering of her heart in her ears as her eyes wandered from his face down his body, taking in the picture of mouth-watering masculinity that presented itself in front of her. He'd worn a suit to the courthouse, playing along with the part of a lovesick man wanting to be married to the love of his life as soon as possible. It fit him way too well, the fabric accentuating the planes of his body and enhancing his handsome features to next-level gorgeous.

Her mouth dried, and she had to swallow hard to bring clarity back into her thoughts. To her dismay, Rafael noticed her lingering stare, for his smile softened to something more delicate, more primal as his eyes narrowed on her before they fell onto her mouth for a second before coming back up to hold her stare.

The gentle heat the memory of their kiss had ignited flared up, radiating through her body in a sensual and highly inappropriate shudder that had her toes curling in her shoes. Despite knowing that this could never go anywhere, something inside her shifted when she saw her reaction reflected in his face.

He sensed something too.

The thought made her breath catch in her throat, and panic followed the mounting desire, quickly overtaking it, so Maria grabbed her bag and spun away from the image of Rafael to turn towards the bed. Putting her things on the white quilt, she took a few moments to breathe in and out while staring at the wall.

Maria cleared her throat, willing the thickness coating her vocal cords away. Behind her she could hear Rafael taking deep breaths as well. They grew quiet for some time before he said, 'My family believes that eventually fame will come to them. They just have to throw enough money at the problem. They have been circling around me since I left university, urging me to get married and help them. They arranged several matches with suitable women and went as far as sabotaging genuine relationships.'

The whisper of fabric filled the still air as he shifted, and Maria dared to turn around to face him again. She had not expected to get an answer to her earlier question.

Rafael was sitting upright now, slightly bent over with his face resting in his hands for a moment. When he looked back up, a hollowness had replaced the calm from moments ago.

Whatever they had done to him still hurt so badly that it was plainly written on his face.

The instinct to comfort took over. Before she could think of how wise such closeness with Rafael could be, she kneeled before him and rested her hand on his knee. His towering height forced her to tilt her head upward to look at him, her breath once again stuttering when those warm hazel eyes focused on her.

'That's why you don't believe in marriage? Because it would make it too easy for them to get your money?' That didn't sound like a good reason to swear off happiness. Surely there were protections in place for such a case?

'No.' He breathed that word out, his chest deflating as he let out the air he'd sucked in, and the tension around his shoulders slowly dissolved.

Then he sat up so his elbows didn't rest on his knees any more. Slowly, as if time had stopped for a few heartbeats, he leaned forward as the lines around his eyes softened, giving way to a gentle smile. His left hand came up, his fingers curled so that his knuckles brushed along her cheek in a gesture so wrapped in affection that it trembled through Maria.

The air became charged, every breath harder to swallow as a million different signals fired in her brain, bringing a myriad sensations down on her that she had no capacity to process. Not when his cool fingers were touching her so gently.

Then everything inside her ebbed away when his head followed his hand and brushed a tender kiss on her cheek.

'It's sweet how much you care, Maria. Thank you.'

He couldn't tell her, even though the words were right there on the tip of his tongue, just waiting to finally be released into the world. To connect with someone over what had happened to him, how it had changed him as a person. But when he tried to put the hurt into words his chest seized, forcing any air in his lungs to remain inside and giving him no breath to speak.

Rafael just couldn't. It would be inviting Maria into a place inside him that no one had ever seen before—and no one ever would.

That required trust, and it was that kind of trust that he'd learned to withhold, thanks to the damage his family had done to him. If he hadn't trusted Laura, his ex-fiancée and his parents' undercover match, she wouldn't have slipped past his defences so easily, almost robbing him of everything he'd worked so hard to achieve. Her whispers had made him reconsider his family's stance, had made him doubt his own sanity around their toxicity. She had wanted him to make peace with them, so when they got married they could become a real family—a value so important in the Latin community.

And a value that she herself had failed to embody when he'd caught her conspiring with his parents, hearing her promise them that she had 'almost turned him around' the day after he had proposed. His heart had broken into a thousand pieces then and there, the tiny fragments scattering in the wind of this betrayal so he could never be so foolish to trust anyone with it ever again.

That included Maria Dias, no matter how much he yearned to place a second kiss on her full, dark lips as a soft peach tone dusted her cheekbones in response to the kiss on her cheek.

Something Rafael knew he shouldn't have done, but he couldn't help himself when he noticed the genuine worry in her eyes. She wasn't asking to prise information out of him. No, she cared about him like a friend would.

He sat up straight as he realised that he was enjoying her blush a lot more than he should, a lot more than would be appropriate for two people who were *just* friends—and he needed to remind himself that their relationship was just that. A friendship and nothing else. Their ruse had removed whatever other possibilities there might have been if he had found the courage to voice his feelings.

'How about we find somewhere to eat? It's been a long day for both of us. Some food will do us good.' Eating was far from Rafael's mind, but it might help them to calm down. Food had always been something they'd bonded over, whether it was a quick dinner in the kitchen after a long day of work, or during the Sunday farmers' market in the town square, where they tried every new food truck that came to the village.

Though whenever they did that they were never alone in a dimly lit room with soft music setting the mood for something entirely different than a friendly dinner.

Okay, maybe an early dinner was a *terrible* idea.

'I…' Maria started, getting to her feet. He could see the thoughts racing behind her eyes, a sight he didn't get to witness very often. It was her gift for making decisions on the fly that made her such an excellent vet in emergencies, her hand acting the moment she identified a problem.

Her delicate and capable hands. How would they feel running up and down his bare back, clawing into his shoulders as he…?

'Sure, that sounds like a…good idea.'

Rafael breathed out a thankful sigh as she interrupted his lewd train of thought, for his heart began pumping blood in all the wrong places.

'Good,' he said, and got to his feet as well, clearing his throat to chase away the phantoms of his fantasies. 'Let me get into something more comfortable, and we'll go see what's in the area.'

Maria nodded, her expression veiled, and he hoped it was because she was processing her own thoughts rather than seeing the blatant desire written in his eyes as he looked at her.

He locked the bathroom door behind him and pulled at his tie, tossing it at the side of the sink as he undid the first two buttons of his shirt. Then he turned on the tap and splashed cold water on his face to cool himself down—both physically and mentally.

Unbuttoning the shirt, he threw it off with a shrug and grabbed a plain dark blue shirt and some black shorts from his duffel bag, into which he stuffed his tie, shirt and the trousers, before looking back into the mirror and ruffling a hand through his dark brown hair, its unruly waves hard to tame.

His heart still raced from the memory of his kiss on her cheek, a friendly and innocent gesture if it hadn't cost him so much strength not to claim her mouth with his in a sensual re-enactment of their earlier kiss.

Rafael needed to be careful. The walls he'd built to hide away the pain and damage dwelling within him were there because he needed them—for his own sake as well as for anyone who tried to scale the walls.

He couldn't let that happen. Even though he'd caught himself lowering them just to feel her closeness for one moment. This was the one act of attraction he permitted himself to indulge in, and now that the moment had gone he forced himself to go back inside his fortress, where he planned on spending the rest of his life in solitude.

CHAPTER FIVE

THE DAY MARIA got married had turned out a lot stranger than she had anticipated when she had started dreaming about it as a young teen.

Really, the only thing that matched her expectations was the low hum of awareness vibrating through her body as she walked beside her husband, an arm's width of space between them that was narrowing every now and then, getting them close enough that their arms brushed against one another. Each minuscule touch sent bolts of lightning skittering down her nerves, making it hard to focus on the conversation they were having.

They'd had an early dinner at a small restaurant a short walk from the hotel, their conversation staying away from the heavier topics they'd spoken about in their room. Maria now had a better understanding as to what kind of people his family were, and it made her think that they had a lot in common in that area.

Even if the hurt had a different cause, the result remained the same.

'Have you ever been here?' he asked as they walked down the street.

Instead of walking back the way they came, Rafael had suggested a more scenic route that wound itself closer to the edge of the forest. Without the hectic traffic of the main street, they could hear the insects chirping and see fireflies coming to life as the sun dropped beneath the horizon, casting a soft purple glow onto the city and the adjacent trees.

'Yes, every now and then I come down here for a case or the occasional workshop with other vets.' Due to its proximity to the rainforest, Manaus was the perfect base for the federal institute for veterinary medicine. What Maria did on a smaller scale—rescuing injured wild animals and rehabilitating them back into the wild—happened here in much larger numbers.

'You come all the way here to consult on cases?' Rafael asked, his gaze still trailing the edge of the forest, a fascinated expression on his face.

'Rarely, but yes. I studied here, as did Celine, so we have a lot of contacts here that we've kept in touch with over the years. My sister is somewhat of a protégée in the vet circles here, so even though I don't have nearly as many accolades as her, they still come with the occasional questions when it comes to rare reptiles they're dealing with.' Unfortunately for reptiles, they were rarely the favourite pets her fellow vets wanted to deal with, even though their healthcare needed specialised attention and compassion. Though dogs, cats and rabbits tugged on her heartstrings whenever they came in, it was the snakes and lizards that needed her help the most.

Even the most harmless of snakes would strike terror in someone unfamiliar with them, so a lot of the snakes brought into her clinic were injured by fearful humans who didn't know any better—or didn't care to learn.

'I thought Celine was a bit…young, but I didn't want to assume anything from just looking at her,' Rafael said.

'She is incredibly smart and, coupled with the stubbornness of an old mule, there isn't a single thing she couldn't achieve if she sets her mind to it.' Maria smiled, a familiar warmth rising in her chest as she thought about her baby sister. 'Celine was so gifted growing up, she graduated high school early and started university while I was still there.' Something that had fused those two sisters together, forging an unbreakable bond that lasted to this day.

Whatever life threw at them, Maria knew they would deal with it together. Like the crisis they were dealing with right now.

'They had never seen such a young student at the school—she was only seventeen. I was in the final year of my doctorate when she joined,' she continued, smiling at the memory of their time together. 'All of us thought she would go into research or become the state veterinarian overseeing the institute here in Manaus. But instead, she chose to stay in our little village and run our parents' charity with me and our brother, Daniel.'

Rafael tore his gaze from the treeline to look at her, his expression one of surprise.

'But if Celine is that young, she must have had Nina when she was in her early twenties?'

Maria nodded, remembering the day she'd found out about Celine's pregnancy—along with the less desirable news that her husband, Darius, had left without any trace or word. Though Nina was her niece, she felt like a second mother to the little girl, filling in whenever Celine was busy and making sure she had everything she needed.

'It was quite the shock for both of us, but we pulled through. Celine didn't have anyone else to rely on and so we decided to raise her together. When Mirabel came along, I had at least *some* skills in motherhood to be more comfortable.' Her words skated over the hardships they'd faced, but those memories of her and her sister were fond ones. They had struggled, yes, but knowing both Nina and Mirabel, having those two girls in her life was worth any struggle ten times over.

'How did Mirabel come to live with you? I suspected you must have another sibling, but I didn't know you had a brother,' Rafael said in a casual tone, not knowing the wound he was prodding at. Even though they had grown close over the last three months, she had stayed away from anything relating to Daniel.

The smile faded at the memory of her brother, the taste in her mouth turning to ash. How could he have done that to her, after she had paused so much of her life to keep the family legacy going? He'd left because he'd fallen in love, not realising that Maria too had that yearning—and had chosen to focus on her family first.

'Because oftentimes I pretend like I don't,' Maria said, surprised by the sharpness in her voice. 'He wasn't a vet like Celine and me. He went to school for business to help us run the charity from that angle, maybe even grow it beyond what we were doing back then.'

She paused, a wry smile pulling at her lips.

'He was the one who initially wanted to introduce a general vet practice to increase our funds, but I refused because I didn't want to bring an outsider into our charity. Sometimes I wonder what he would think that his actions forced me to implement an idea we fought about so often.'

'Where is he now?'

Wasn't that the question? Maria hesitated, her tongue darting over her lips and wetting them. Where had the superficial conversation gone? No one knew the circumstances of Daniel's disappearance, and Maria had never wanted to tell anyone—the fear of being judged scaring her away from any such conversation.

But Rafael somehow made it easy. The noncommittal banter as well as the heartfelt conversation—they both seemed to go so much easier with him.

'He ran away with the woman he was having an affair with. We had a wealthy donor who had picked our charity as his focus when we saved his daughter. She had suffered a snake bite while they were hiking nearby. Given my work, I always have the antidote for most local snakes around, so we were able to help her when they rushed into town to call for help.

'Daniel got too close to his wife and they...

fell in love. So he left with her, and with him went the donation we depended on. Mirabel is his daughter. He left her too, when he ran.'

Just saying these words out loud was surreal, the story sounding made up.

She glanced at Rafael, whose thoughtful expression had given way to something much stonier. Then he asked, 'He left his daughter behind with not a second thought as to what that would do to her—and you?'

The intensity in his voice took her by surprise, his eyes darkening, but not with the attraction she swore she had seen on his face when he had kissed her cheek. No, this was on the other side of the primal spectrum, her hurt somehow triggering something within him.

Or was she reading too much into the situation? Reading too much into that kiss as well?

'I—'

A soft whining interrupted her, a noise Maria had heard so often it triggered a response without hesitation.

She stopped dead in her tracks, her finger raised to her lips as she strained her ears to hear the direction the noise had come from. Rafael raised his eyebrows in a silent question, but his eyes went wide when the noise sounded again, pulling them towards the path on their right, leading to a narrow gap between houses.

There, in the middle of the alley, stood a small monkey, its open mouth producing the same whining noise they had just heard.

'Is this a…?'

'A tamarin monkey,' Maria finished, taking a hesitant step forward and crouching down to look at the squirrel-sized monkey. Its white fur curled like a moustache around its mouth, giving it a sentient air as it blinked with intelligent eyes.

'They stay in the city?' Rafael asked, to which she nodded.

'They have to. With all the urban development happening in recent years, the city cut more and more into the monkeys' territories. They could have fled inland, but they soon realised that the city was a perfect hunting ground for food—what with all the humans throwing things away.'

'This one seems to be behaving oddly.'

'It is…'

Maria got back up and took another step towards the monkey. It stilled as it beheld the two humans, head slightly cocked. Then it turned around, running a few paces down the road before it stopped again, looking at them with another low cry.

Maria and Rafael exchanged questioning

glances. 'I think it's asking us to follow it,' he said, scepticism lacing every word.

Scepticism that Maria didn't quite share. She'd worked with enough monkeys to understand their inherent intelligence, their adaptability to changing circumstances something to marvel at. The tamarin monkeys were a perfect example of that. It had taken them only a few years to adapt to urban life within the city.

Together they stepped forward and when they got close enough to the monkey it turned around again, leading them down the street until they spotted another monkey lying on the floor.

Maria's vet instincts kicked in immediately, and so must have Rafael's for she felt him tense up next to her and they crossed the remaining distance at a sprint. Two smaller monkeys sat close to the one lying prone on the floor—likely their parent. Its eyes were open, but its breath shallow by the look of its chest, only rising with agonising slowness.

'What happened?' Maria asked no one in particular as she knelt down, brushing away the remains of a half-eaten sandwich and some other food waste that the other adult monkey had collected—no doubt in an endeavour to help its mate.

She patted down her trousers, searching for her phone, when a light above her shoulder clicked on. Turning her head, she watched as Rafael knelt beside her with his phone in his hand, shining down on the family of tamarin monkeys so they could assess the extent of the injury.

With the light shining, it took Maria all but one glance to see what had happened to the monkey. Its leg lay stretched out at an unnatural angle, old blood crusting its fur. Somehow it had got its leg stuck in something and had ripped the skin open when trying to escape, likely breaking a bone. In the rainforest such a misstep would have meant its demise, but with their new urban lifestyle the monkeys faced a far more painful death removed from any circle of life.

Not if they could help it. Maria shot Rafael a sideways glance. 'I have an animal first aid kit in my bag at the hotel. Can you run and get it while I assess the situation? We need to get all these monkeys to a clinic.'

Rafael nodded, handing her his phone, which she propped up against the wall so she could approach the injured animals with caution. She didn't have any protective gear on her, no long sleeves or thick gloves to ward off any bites that an injured and frightened monkey could resort to.

'You did good in alerting us,' she said to the monkey that had led them here. It was waiting a few steps further along, eyeing her. 'I can help you.'

She leaned forward with deliberate slowness, her hands stretched in front of her and open so they could all see her palms and understand she meant no harm. When she finally got closer, she reached out her hand and leaned over the injured tamarin monkey, careful not to touch it until she was done with her visual examination.

'Are you their mother?' Maria asked in a soothing tone that she had learned put frightened animals at ease. From looking at her belly and her teats, she could see that the mother monkey was still breastfeeding her young.

They must not have eaten since their mother had collapsed. Their stress levels must be through the roof right now, but even then, the other monkey had realised that they needed intervention from a higher power. Very curious how the urbanisation worked for them, she thought to herself.

'I think you got your leg caught somewhere and when you strained to break free, you damaged a bone and tore your skin open.' She liked to explain the procedure to the animal as she was tending to them. While she knew they didn't understand anything she said, it helped them to hear someone speak to them.

'Once Rafael gets back, we will see if we can figure out your break and splint it to transport you to the clinic where I used to study.' She lifted her head to look at the young monkeys and the father. 'You can all come too. Once Mum is better, you'll be released back into the forest.'

Hurried footsteps echoed behind her, prompting her to release a sigh of relief as, a few moments later, Rafael came to a halt next to her, handing her the first aid kit. Years of working on the road had built the habit to bring the very basic equipment she needed with her, no matter where she went.

Rafael's eyebrows shot up when he put the bag down and watched her unzip it. She'd called it a kit, but he thought it was more akin to a miniature veterinarian clinic than a simple first aid kit as he saw the contents. Stethoscope, gloves, gauze, thermometer, and even a variety of oral medication and ointments were in the bag, giving them everything they needed to help this animal in need until they could get them to a safe place. The clinic, she had said, but what exactly that place was Rafael wasn't sure. She didn't mean the federal institute for veterinary medicine, did she?

Maria had said that she was familiar with some people there, but could they just walk into a government agency like that?

Wherever they would end up going, he was glad she was here to lend her expertise. Each veterinarian learned about a breadth of animals, but never as much as about the ones they chose to specialise in. For Rafael that had been dogs, cats and small animals typically found to be people's pets. While he knew enough about animals in general to help with simple ailments, anything beyond surface level needed an expert in more exotic animal care.

An expert like Maria Dias.

He had to admit that he'd only looked her up after he'd accepted the job at her charity just because he'd wanted to learn more about what it did and what he would be a part of. He wasn't prepared for the praise and accolades from different animal rescue organisations that her charity had worked with.

A couple of hours ago she had called her sister Celine a protégée, completely downplaying her own effort when it came to rescuing and rehabilitating the wildlife of the rainforest which fell victim to constructions and deforestation.

It was that compassion and care that went beyond the call of duty that had drawn him to her after a few days of working with her. While Rafael cared for animals just as much as she did, the thought that he was treating someone's family member kept him humble and hardworking, wanting to make sure that they got the very best of care.

Maria, on the other hand, became the family member of the animals that wound up in her care, because there was no one else to care for them. Just like she was demonstrating right now as she pulled the latex gloves over her hands and handed him his own pair to put on.

He obliged, waiting on the sidelines for any instructions she might give. In this situation he was no more than her assistant, helping her with whatever she needed to get that monkey back to full health.

'The injured monkey looks to be female, gave birth probably two months ago judging by the size of her babies.' Rafael nodded, even though he could tell she was mostly talking to herself. A habit they shared, as he liked to record his examinations so he could play them back later to take patient notes.

'What are our next steps?' he asked when Maria remained quiet.

'I'll try to touch her and see from there,' she said, and reached out a careful hand.

The young monkeys looked at her with wide eyes, one of them baring its teeth as she got closer, but neither them nor the adult monkey a few paces behind them moved. They all watched as she laid a tentative hand on the female monkey, gently stroking her with a cooing noise.

'Okay, we are good to go to the next step. Let's get her on some painkillers before we inspect her leg. There will still be discomfort, but at least we can lessen it somewhat. Can you see a bottle labelled ketoprofen in the bag?'

Rafael picked up several bottles, reading their labels, before he found the medication she mentioned. He glanced at the tiny monkey, the adult one not much larger than a squirrel, and picked the smallest syringe available.

'How much?' he asked as he poked the thin needle through the cork of the bottle to pull some of the solution out.

Maria took a second to look at the monkey, tilting her head left and right as if she was trying to get a good measure of the animal before she said, 'I don't think she weighs more than a kilo, so let's go with two millilitres, and remember to note that when we bring her in.'

He nodded, then drew the small amount of liquid into the syringe and handed it to Maria. She took it from him, pausing a moment before taking some of the monkey's skin between her fingers and injecting the medication subcutaneously and giving it a few moments before she handed the syringe back to him.

Rafael dug around the kit and found some bags marked for biohazardous waste and dropped the syringe in there before clamping it shut. Then he took out a small spray bottle that he assumed was either filled with water or saline solution, and a medical wipe, handing her both just as she opened her mouth to say something.

She closed her lips and the smile that appeared on them knocked the air out of his lungs, not because of her feminine sensuality that lay underneath every one of her moves, but the sheer purity of the moment as they worked together to help an injured animal. Even though they worked in the same spaces, their paths rarely crossed. Now they had finally got to share such a moment shifted something inside him, changing something within him he wasn't sure he wanted changed.

It went beyond the professional admiration

he had for her, and tapped into the hesitant flirting they had indulged in over the three months he'd been working for her charity, always in the secure knowledge that the words, the glances and the smiles would never go anywhere beyond what they were. They were only ever supposed to be friends.

But this… Seeing her compassion and skill in action was an experience he'd never thought would impact him as much as it did right now. He wanted more of it in his life, more of *her*.

All those thoughts flashed through his mind in a matter of seconds as their eyes locked, her gloved fingers grazing his when she took the items from him. Then she tore her gaze away from him, leaving him with sudden vertigo as his consciousness crashed back into reality. What had just happened?

The monkey whines were barely audible as Maria sprayed the solution in the bottle onto the mangled leg and carefully wiped it clean of the crusted blood that covered the fur. He handed her another wipe when the one in her hand became caked in blood and this time she accepted it without looking at him, her full attention on their patient in front of them.

'You're doing so great, mama monkey. I can see you have some cuts on your upper thigh that are looking a bit infected. I'm going to see if I can figure out where else you hurt your leg,' she said to the animal, then she gently lifted the leg to slide one of her hands underneath it, probing the flesh with gentle fingers.

She squeezed her eyes shut as her hands worked up and down the leg, only ever pressing as much as she needed to understand what lay beneath the skin, a skill Rafael admired in her. Under normal circumstances they would get an X-ray of the injured area to look at it on a film and take any of the guesswork out of it.

Though he had never really thought about it until this moment, he understood now that this was a luxury she oftentimes didn't have if she was out in the rainforest responding to a call the locals had put in to alert her of an injured animal requiring help. At least on a first pass she needed to figure out what was wrong so she could stabilise her patients and get them to the clinic.

'I think she broke her tibia,' she said when she opened her eyes again. 'She probably needs a splint to keep from moving, but I can't do that here without a way to see what the break looks like. If I set it now the bones might not line up enough to promote a clean heal.'

Rafael nodded. 'So we need to bring her to the clinic. Any idea how we can transport all of them?'

Though Maria travelled around with a small veterinary surgery in her pocket, he knew that she didn't have a carrier she could put the monkeys in. She sighed as she looked around, no doubt thinking the same thing.

'Let me call the clinic and see if they can pick us up,' she said, letting go of the monkey's leg but keeping her left hand on its stomach in a reassuring pat as she peeled the glove off her right hand and took her phone out of her back pocket.

'Come on, pick up your phone,' she whispered after several rings, and Rafael felt the relief he saw washing over her face in his own body when the call finally connected.

Rafael lay on the couch, the room veiled in darkness, and listened to the steady stream of the shower sounding down the hall. His chest tightened at the thought of Maria standing under the water, dark brown skin glistening as tiny drops pearled down her delicate throat and collarbone and then…

He shook his head, banishing the unwanted images into a place inside him where he could lock them up and forget about them. Because that was what he needed to do in this situation. Forget about the alluring femininity and grace that had showed in every one of her movements as she'd examined the helpless tamarin monkey they'd found in the alley.

After calling her friend at the federal institute, a car had come to pick up the monkey and its family in a carrier, and the vet had assured Maria that all would be taken care of. She'd hovered for a second back then, making Rafael think that she might be invested enough to jump into the car with the other vet to see to the treatment of the monkey herself. But then she'd stepped back, letting them take the family of four away, and they'd walked back to the hotel in silence.

Rafael's stomach still roiled from the information she'd shared with him, letting him see the depth of her hurt, and his own wounds had responded in a way he hadn't anticipated, hadn't wanted them to either. What had happened with his family, with Laura, didn't concern anyone but himself. Everything would stay locked behind the thick walls he'd built.

Walls Maria seemed to dance around as if they weren't tall and imposing.

It was the compassion he'd witnessed within her tonight that had cracked open those ancient bricks hiding away his fear, daring to shine some light into the fissures—a light coming from her and the depth of care she'd given those monkeys.

It made him proud to work for her, work with the charity that facilitated such necessary acts every single day. But it was also seeing her live by the values she preached at her donors. She wasn't just a pretty face—and dear God, what a stunningly pretty face that was. No, she also cared so deeply that it put everyone else to shame in comparison.

That was a good reason to give her his money, though he still carried some hesitation in his chest. Throughout the day he'd watched his back, looking every stranger they encountered over twice while leaning into their fake romance as much as possible. If his family was sniffing around—and he had no doubt that was happening—they would go to great lengths to invalidate his marriage if they even as much as suspected that it wasn't genuine. It was the one risk that could blow up this whole plan. If they found out they weren't married the way his grandparents had meant for him to be married, they could hold up the money in a drawn-out legal battle. The charity couldn't afford that if it wanted to stay open. They needed access to his trust as soon as possible.

But what was he supposed to do? He had no idea what married life would look like for them once they were back in Santarém. They already lived together since his contract included her guest room free of charge. They had their daily routines, like having coffee together while talking about the previous day's cases, or dinner with Celine and the girls.

Would any of that remain, now that they had altered their relationship irrevocably? If he was honest with himself, Rafael hadn't really thought beyond this point when he'd come up with the ruse.

Or the fact that the attraction he sensed zipping between them when he looked at her a fraction too long was genuine. No, he'd thought this was no more than a fleeting infatuation for a man who had long since given up on love and any physical intimacy with it.

The trickling of the water stopped, snapping him out of his contemplations and catapulting him back into the room. He listened to her shuffling footsteps and, a moment later, the door opened. The bathroom light shining from the back obscured everything but Maria's silhouette, a shadow of curves and sensuality that summoned a rush of blood to his groin. Then the light went off, and his eyes needed a moment to adjust to the complete darkness until he could see in the gentle moonlight that filtered through the slats of the blinds.

Maria must have seen his open eyes for she smiled at him before she sat on the bed, her eyes darting between him and some invisible point on the wall only she could see.

In the dim light of the moon she looked absolutely striking, her dark skin deepening and highlighting what he knew to be velvety sweet to the touch. He swallowed the lump appearing in his throat, his thoughts turning to the unbridled desire he'd been staving off for months now.

It had been building throughout their friendship, so subtly that he didn't even realise how much he'd grown attached to her emotionally—on a human level. Though he'd been attracted to other women, the desire never ran so deep, the urge to conquer so all-consuming that he could think of little else in her presence. It was the kind of passion that came on the back of a more important emotional connection.

And it struck fear in his heart.

'Did I wake you?' Maria said, her voice just above a whisper as if she was afraid to wake him, when sleep was the furthest from his mind. How could he sleep with this fire of desire burning in the pit of his stomach? With the fear that came along with it that he had slipped too deep into this deception already?

'No, I was still awake,' he simply said, propping his head up on the couch so he could get a better look at her, and immediately regretting it when the heat contained in his belly spread like a wildfire to every remote corner of his body.

She wore an oversized shirt with a faded print he couldn't make out from his position, and a pair of linen shorts that hid just enough of her curves that his mind went wild imagining what lay underneath the tantalising strip of cloth. Even in scrubs Rafael hadn't been able to keep his eyes off her, his gaze following her around whenever he thought she wasn't watching—sometimes getting caught with a smile and wink.

There was no wink now as his eyes roamed over her, following the curve of her long legs that vanished under the thin covering, before going back up her body. Her chest rose and fell in an uneven pattern, her breasts pushing against the fabric of her shirt, and between the flecks of print on the shirt he saw the tips of her nipples straining against it.

His eyes darted to her face as heat exploded through his body again, bringing his blood to an impossible boil. From the wide-eyed expression on her face, he could glimpse that her body's reaction was as involuntary as his. Neither of them *wanted* to be in the situation they currently found themselves.

'Are you sure you'll be okay on the couch? It looks a bit short,' she said with a gentle clearing of her throat.

'I'll be fine. It's only a couple of hours and then we'll be back in Santarém.'

Maria hesitated for a moment, then she said, 'I don't mind if you want to be more comfortable.'

Rafael blinked slowly. He needed a few seconds to process what she had just said, because it certainly couldn't be what his lewd brain was telling him it was. No, this was his lust reading into a perfectly innocent statement.

This was not an invitation to anything other than a restful night.

Rafael shook his head, knowing his voice might betray his desire. Instead, he opted to change the subject.

'That was some quick thinking today. I don't think the mother or her babies would have made it without your intervention,' he said, recalling a part of their day that was safe to talk about.

Maria smiled again, a lot brighter than a moment ago, and her white teeth showed in stark contrast to the darkness swallowing her as the night progressed. Rafael shifted around for a moment, both to escape the heat her gaze was searing through him with what could only be described as an innocent smile, and to look through the blinds up into the sky.

The moon had dipped below the tree line of the rainforest, whose ancient branches reached high up, almost enveloping them in a canopy of green. Though Manaus was built to be a gateway into the Amazon and its beauty, the glow of the city still polluted the sky, dimming out the light of the stars. Though he'd lived in Brazil his entire life, he'd only once been to a place remote enough to see the stars in their full glory.

'What was it like growing up with famous grandparents?' Maria asked into the quiet, drawing his attention back to her.

'What?' he asked in return, the question dropping deep into the memories of his subconscious and only slowly resurfacing.

'You said they were part of *Patas Para O Amor*, right? There's hardly a *novela* that is more popular than that one, especially in vet circles. Did that impact your decision to become a vet as well?'

Rafael blinked a few times, trying to untangle the painful emotions from the few happy ones he knew lay within him. Something outside of the trauma his parents had inflicted—the trauma his grandparents' money had contributed to—that he could share with her. Because he *wanted* to share something of his. Something that wasn't all doom and gloom, but something light. Something she could appreciate about him, and yes, maybe even find attractive. Though why he wanted to appeal to her, he didn't know. Other than that hunger within him that wanted—*needed*—to be close to her in any way he could.

'I think they showed me the possibility, yes. By the time my nanny brought me to the farm on a daily basis I knew the concept of a vet. Though by the time I was old enough to make this decision, they had already passed away. I give them a bit of credit, but most of it goes to Camila and her family's animals.'

He paused before he continued. 'The show had stopped before I was even born, but the memory of their achievements were very prominent in our house and they spoke a lot about how *Patas Para O Amor* helped the family become what it was. So maybe in a way they inspired me?' He shrugged, the memories pouring from his lips as if they had just been waiting for Maria to arrive so he could finally share what had been buried inside him for years.

'I always had an affinity for animals,' he said with a chuckle that vibrated through Maria's body all the way down to her bones. 'The person everyone thought was my best friend in high school only hung out with me because his parents had got a dog for him, and he was tired of taking care of it. So I became the dog's caretaker and took him with me when I left for university.'

Maria smiled at that. Even back then he had volunteered his own time to help an animal who needed him. It was a trait she'd noticed in him when he'd started working at her clinic. Many times she'd found him there late at night because a panicked owner had swung by at an ungodly hour. More often than not the owners were making a big deal out of nothing, but Rafael always took their fear at face value. He understood that these were family members and that sometimes people didn't think rationally when it came to their loved ones.

'You didn't have your own pets?' she asked, surprised at that. In *Patas Para O Amor* they'd worked with a lot of show animals, so she had been certain their own home would be full of animals as well.

But Rafael shook his head. 'Outside of the horde of barn cats that considered me their king? No, sadly not. Maybe that's why my parents thought I couldn't be serious about my plans to become a vet.'

His voice was strained, and Maria sat up just a bit straighter at that. 'They didn't approve?'

A strange concept in her mind. Even though she frowned upon it, she knew that society didn't place a high value on vets, thinking that they *only* worked with animals. None of them considered how much harder it was to treat the medical condition of a living being that couldn't articulate where it hurt. *They* had to be the ones so tuned in to the animals' well-being that they could sense and understand their various ailments.

Rafael shook his head, his lips pressed into a thin line that she yearned to soothe away with her fingers. His help with the injured monkey had been so invaluable today, and he hadn't even hesitated for a second, knowing exactly why she needed to help—and giving her the space to do so. In a professional capacity she had dealt with many vets, talented people who sometimes couldn't step away when someone with more expertise took charge of a situation.

He'd been nothing like that, yielding to her requests as she'd sent him off to fetch her first aid kit so they could patch up the monkey well enough for transport to the clinic to arrive.

This evening would be one she'd remember

for a long time after they parted ways. That thought caused another twinge in her chest, making her swallow hard as things within her surfaced that she didn't want to, didn't have the space inside her to process.

She absolutely could not be this attracted to Rafael. It was bordering on self-destructive insanity that her hands twitched with the need to smooth away the worry lines appearing around his eyes and the corners of his mouth. Longing gripped her, radiating tantalising warmth through her body, and Maria had to admit that she had lost control over her mounting desire for this man.

'No, they didn't approve. The one thing my parents always wanted, above anything else, was the fame and acknowledgement that my grandparents got for their work in the field of television. With the fortune his parents gave my father upon marrying my mother they founded a media company so they could recreate *Patas Para O Amor*, hoping that the family name would carry them along. It did, and that was their demise when it came to turning promises into action.' Rafael sighed and his head rolled backwards against his cushion so he was staring up at the ceiling.

Maria remembered the reboot of her beloved *novela* and how she'd watched two episodes before turning it off for ever. It just didn't have that magical feeling of the original, but she'd always thought it was her not being able to appreciate the reboot for what it was through her thick nostalgia goggles. Rafael seemed to suggest the production really was inferior.

'They ran out of money quickly, which is when they turned to my siblings and me to see if we wanted to *invest* in their company. Both my brother and sister had been raised as fame-hungry socialites, so they jumped at that opportunity, and they too put all their trust money into my parents' company at the chance of being a part of the show.'

Maria frowned, the quiet pain in his voice like a knife cutting through her. 'You don't have a relationship with your siblings either?'

He'd alluded to this when they'd spoken earlier, his discomfort around his family clear even as they'd planned this ruse back in her clinic.

He shook his head. 'They chose to accept the arranged matches from our parents—the children of other executives in the entertainment industry. I might have been able to set my differences with them aside if they weren't just as bad as my parents when it came to my trust.'

'They were also pressuring you into things you didn't want?' she asked, a shiver shaking her.

She was so close to her own sister, their lives so intertwined that she couldn't imagine not being a part of her life—or be so different from her that she couldn't.

'Pretty much. They would do whatever they were commanded to do by our parents. I thought I could trust them at one point, until...'

His voice trailed off and Maria strained to hear the rest of the sentence, but he didn't reveal anything else.

Not that he needed to. Today Maria had learned a lot more about his family and was appalled at their behaviour. They would put their children, people they'd promised to protect, through financial ruin, just at a chance of fame and riches? It sounded absurd, especially since it sounded as if they were already very well-off with the money from their trusts. Why risk it all for something so vapid and insubstantial?

'And now you are the only remaining Pedro child to hold out?' she asked, and he gave her a slow nod, his eyes still searching something invisible on the ceiling.

'They almost got me too. For years they

tried to match me with people they thought would bring an advantageous family connection. Daughters of other media moguls or wealthy personalities in Brazil. When I turned them all down, they eventually stopped. And then Laura appeared out of nowhere, as if sent by some higher power, and I…' His voice trailed off again, and it was only then that Maria noticed she had been holding her breath in anticipation of his confession. Even in the dim moonlight she could see the pain etched into every feature of his handsome face that normally shone with compassion and kindness. It seemed so wrong to only see hurt and bitterness reflected in it now.

Was that what he'd wanted to say a few moments ago? Had his siblings been involved with this Laura as well?

He cleared his throat, and the thickness in his voice was apparent. Whatever had happened with this woman had changed him for ever in some way. Was that why he didn't believe in love any more? Because his attempts had failed?

Maria almost prompted him to finish his sentence but closed her lips again when he shook his head. She'd never seen him so torn up and it took a considerable amount of her willpower to keep sitting where she was when everything within her wanted to get close to him and hug him tight, kiss the pain away. Let him kiss her pain away too…

'We should sleep. The flight leaves early tomorrow, and we'll have to be on our best behaviour.' These was an undertone to his words that Maria struggled to understand.

What did he mean by that? That he sensed what was going on between them and was reminding her that it was all off-limits? Did that mean he felt it too, the attraction brewing between them since they'd started working together?

Her mind ran in circles around this one sentence, analysing the myriad meanings his words could have, and drawing up short on all of them.

So she just nodded, sinking down into her pillows when his strained voice sounded once again. *'Boa noite.'*

CHAPTER SIX

MARIA WOKE UP to the scent of food wafting up her nose. She squeezed her eyes shut, turning around in her bed, trying to find her way back to sleep. But the smell of burnt toast had her open one eye to look at the alarm clock on her nightstand. Barely past eight and Celine was already destroying their kitchen? Since when did her sister bother to cook anyway? Most of the time this woman lived off nothing but black coffee and the occasional piece of fruit.

With a groan Maria forced herself out of bed, the motivation that her sister might burn their house down if left unattended in the kitchen enough to wake her up. Celine must have just arrived home. Her specialty as a livestock vet meant she serviced a lot of farms in the surrounding area, oftentimes needing to attend them for the calf and foal season to supervise the trickier births. Those couldn't be scheduled so that meant her sister had to attend whenever they happened—even when it was the middle of the night.

She hesitated in front of her dresser and looked down on herself. Should she get dressed before leaving her room? That question had never entered her mind before she and Rafael had entered into their ruse. What was now different that she didn't want him to see her like that?

Maria's pulse stumbled as it accelerated, and she forced herself to open her door and step outside. Relief mingled with something else far deeper and more primal within her as her eyes fell on Rafael's closed door. He wasn't up yet. Good. She needed a moment alone with her sister to talk about what had happened in the last week.

She stepped out of her room and glanced through the door next to hers into her nieces' room. Nina's bed was empty, no doubt *helping* her mother prepare breakfast downstairs, but Mirabel sat at her desk, headphones on as she quietly drew on a piece of paper.

'Bom dia, amor,' Maria said loud enough so her niece would hear her through the headphones.

She looked up from her artwork and pushed the headphones off her ears. *'Bom dia, Tia,'* she said with a small smile that made an ache bloom in her chest.

After all that had happened to her, she seemed so calm when Maria knew that her father abandoning her must still hurt, even after so much time. Maria and Celine had tried to get in touch with their brother, urging him to come back, not for them but for his daughter, promising that they would forget what had happened and that it wasn't about the money. But Daniel had never replied, never even asked about his child and how she was doing. It was that callousness that turned the blood in her veins into raging lava. How could he have done that to his little girl, all for a woman he'd met a couple of times? The *love of his life* as he had put it in that pathetic excuse of a goodbye note for her and Celine.

'Your *tia* is making food for us. Are you coming downstairs?'

Mirabel made a face that reflected the feelings Maria herself had about Celine's cooking. 'I had cereal when I woke up,' she said, her nose crinkling as the smell of burning food intensified around them.

'Solid choice. Maybe it's not too late for me to do that as well.' Her niece chuckled, transforming the thunderous rage in her chest into a warm sensation of unconditional love for the child who had become her daughter in everything but name. 'Okay, let me help your aunt before she renders us all homeless because of an uncontrolled kitchen fire.'

Mirabel put her headphones back on, and Maria hurried downstairs, inspecting the scene as she rounded the corner into the kitchen.

Celine stood half turned from the stove, scraping way too hard at a substance in the pan that resembled scrambled eggs but didn't quite have the right colour or texture to be considered that. The pieces of bread sticking out of the toaster were almost black. The expression on her younger sister's face was one of pure concentration as she squinted at her phone propped up against the wall on the kitchen counter. Was she reading a recipe for scrambled eggs?

The entire scene was so bizarre, Maria couldn't stop her laughter from erupting, prompting Celine to whirl around to look at her in surprise.

'What do you think you're doing, *bebê*?' she asked, propping her hands on her hips as she beheld the utter chaos that reigned in her kitchen. 'You know you can't cook.'

'I can perform surgery on a newborn rabbit, I should be able to make scrambled eggs,' Celine replied, though the glance at the pan in her hand didn't convey any of her false bravado. 'Anyway, this isn't for you. This is for… Alexander.'

At the mention of his name, the Great Dane raised his head in question, bumping against the dangling feet of her other niece, Nina, who sat on a comfy armchair with a tablet in her hand, watching something flashing on the screen.

'I promise you even he won't eat that.' Maria stepped closer and snapped her fingers, summoning the large dog to her side before snatching the pan out of her sister's hands and presenting it to him. Alexander looked inside the pan, sniffing at its contents and then raising his snout at her with another questioning look.

'See? He doesn't even interpret it as real food,' she said with a laugh, Celine's expression turning thunderous.

'I'm never going to do *anything* nice for you ever again,' she hissed, before leaving the house to throw the failed attempt at breakfast into the compost bin around the back of the house.

Meanwhile, Maria poured herself a coffee from the already steaming pot. Her sister was so dependent on her caffeine that she knew she could trust her ability to make coffee without hesitation. Then she followed Mirabel's suggestion and poured herself a bowl of cereal just as Celine returned, sitting down on the chair across from her with a still sour expression that made her chuckle.

'Okay, how about I acknowledge that you tried to make breakfast for me, and I'll appreciate the gesture and spirit behind it without actually having consumed any of it.' She sipped on her coffee, its sweet taste chasing away the final remnants of sleep clinging to her. 'And in return you'll tell me why you chose to endanger the kids and me with your cooking.'

Celine scowled, taking a deep drink from her own mug. 'I need a reason to do something nice for my family? I haven't seen you in a while, with all the work going on in the farms. We need to talk.'

There was an undertone in her voice that wasn't lost on Maria. They *had* a lot to talk about, because the last time they'd spoken was the night they'd discussed the demise of their charity at the hands of their brother. She'd told her sister that she needed to fire Rafael and make some arrangements to forward animals in need to a clinic a few hundred kilometres south. That had been almost two weeks ago. *A lot* had changed since then.

'Okay…' Maria nodded, taking a deep breath as she considered where to even start. She and Rafael had come back from Manaus the day after they'd signed their marriage licence. On their way to the airport his lawyer had called, informing him that he'd submitted the papers to the bank, but that it would take at least a month for the funds to be released. A whole month where they needed to pretend they were a married couple on the off-chance that someone came sniffing around them to expose their marriage for the fraud that it was.

Both working and living together had changed since they'd returned back home, their interactions fuelled by the persistent undercurrent of mutual attraction. Somewhere in all of this, she had reached the understanding that the electric charge between them was *very* real and not a figment of her affection-starved imagination.

But their agreement was so simple it almost became complicated again. Their one rule was to make it believable, and Maria knew, from everything he had told her about his family, that everyone around them needed to believe that they were a genuine couple. That meant telling the whole village that they were married, acting like they were in love in front of everyone…

How could she do that to her friends? The people in Santarém were almost a part of her family. They would be so hurt if they found out that Maria had lied to them. Or would they ultimately understand that she had done it to save her sanctuary?

How would the villagers treat Rafael when they found out? He'd been nothing but gentle and kind to her throughout this entire process.

The night in the hotel flashed in her memory whenever she had an unguarded moment, rocking through her with an intensity that was ridiculous. *Nothing* had happened. The flash of a moment where he'd looked her up and down, his thoughts matching the rapid beating of her heart as they'd both admitted to something non-verbally. That their forced kiss had affected him as much as her, and that she wasn't alone in her yearning to repeat it—without the audience this time.

'You probably noticed that Rafael is still here.' She didn't know where exactly to start her story, but this piece of information was as good as any.

Even though they'd agreed that they wouldn't tell anyone that their marriage was fake, Maria had no intention of withholding that information from her sister. She couldn't. The charity was *theirs*. They had each put so much work and passion into it, she needed to know how she was saving it.

'That's one of the things I was wondering about.' Celine paused, smirking. 'Is it because you like him that you couldn't do it? Do I have to be the bad guy?'

Maria flushed, giving her sister exactly the reaction she wanted. 'No, that's not it.' How was she supposed to tell her that she'd got fake married? It was such a strange concept that she could barely articulate it.

'That evening we had an emergency admission, and after we took care of it I spoke to him about our problems. That we had to shut down the charity because we couldn't find enough donations to keep things going, even with the extra cash from the vet services.' She paused, the memory of that evening so fuzzy compared to the vivid details of what had happened since then when they'd travelled to Manaus.

'When he heard that we might close because of financial trouble, he offered to donate some money to buy us more time to look for a permanent donor.' Maria let out a breath when she noticed her voice quietening. So far so good. She could get through the rest of it as well.

Celine raised her eyebrows. 'He has enough money to bankroll us until we can find someone else? Why is he here in Santarém when he has so much money?'

'You remember *Patas Para O Amor*?' she asked, already knowing the answer.

'Of course, how could I not remember?' Celine blinked, clearly trying to make a connection between what she had just heard and that seemingly unrelated question.

'The lead couple from the original were a couple in real life, I don't know if you remember that. Anyway, turns out Rafael is related to them, and owns quite a fortune thanks to the success of his grandparents.'

She stopped, watching Celine carefully as she said each word. Her sister's eyes went wide at that nugget of information, almost making Maria laugh at the absurdity that was about to come out of her mouth next. If she was shocked right now, she would faint when she heard what she was about to share.

'So again, what on earth is he doing here if he is rich?' Celine asked, giving voice to the question that had led her down the road of marriage almost two weeks ago. Two strange weeks where the air around her and Rafael had been changed for ever, the easygoing nature of their friendship replaced with some hot and intense simmering that neither of them wanted to act on for various reasons.

For Maria it was simple enough that she *knew* they weren't compatible, knew that they wanted different things from this life and that they might have attraction and chemistry, but that meant little if their life goals didn't align.

'Well…' A lump appeared in her throat and she grabbed her coffee to mask it, taking a sip of the already cooling liquid.

Celine raised a questioning eyebrow, seeing the gesture for what it was—a strange attempt to stall at what was coming next.

'Turns out his grandparents were rather traditional people so, instead of giving their children and grandchildren money, they set up a trust for each of them so that they could only get the money when certain…conditions were met.'

She took another sip as her sister's eyes narrowed on her. Understanding dawned on her face, though Maria knew there was no way she could have correctly guessed what those conditions were. Or maybe she'd just realised that whatever conditions there were, Maria was the one who could meet them for Rafael and knew they had entered some sort of deal.

'What did you do, M?' she asked straight away, and any hope Maria might have had of pulling out of the conversation was gone.

She swallowed again, willing her voice to

remain steady as she confessed to the scheme she and Rafael had hatched.

'His grandparents wanted the money to go towards keeping the Pedro family name going and whatnot. To ensure that was how the money was used, they put a clause in the trust that required Rafael to be married before he could access any of the funds they left him.'

Maria paused, letting that information float between them and giving her sister some space to process this. Celine remained quiet, looking straight at her with unblinking eyes. Where there had been an expression of scepticism on her face was now a mask of emptiness, not letting her catch a glimpse of whatever her sister was thinking. Though she wanted to interject and potentially overexplain, Maria remained quiet, giving Celine the time she needed to process. Even though she had not directly said it, she had dropped a big bombshell with this information.

Finally, Celine looked down at her mug, clearing her throat. 'Excuse me, I think I still don't understand then. Because it sounds to me as if you are telling me that you *married* him to get the money, which I know you can't have done.'

'Okay, hear me out—'

'Maria, are you serious right now?'

'It was the only way to save our business, Cee!' Maria cringed at her raised voice, and both women looked to the side to check on Nina, who was still staring ahead at her tablet without a care in the world.

It happened every now and then that the sisters had a disagreement, but whenever that happened, they tried to have it out where the children—and, more recently, also Rafael—couldn't hear them. Since neither of the children's fathers were in the picture any more, they'd assumed the role of both parents in their children's lives, and as such they always strived to appear as a team to them.

Celine had got pregnant on her wedding night, when she'd married her then boyfriend in an impulse elopement that Maria hadn't known about—only for her husband to vanish off the face of the earth a few days later without even a note as to what had happened. They'd eventually found out that he had left Brazil to return to his home country of Peru, though any attempts at contacting him had gone unanswered. Which meant that he didn't even know about his four-year-old daughter.

It was also the reason Maria knew her sister would be very sensitive to her getting married without saying a word about it. Even though it had happened almost five years ago, the wound remained at surface level, making Celine skittish to the concept of marriage, no matter the intention.

She lowered her voice before she continued. 'I know you have strong feelings about people getting married, but this is purely for convenience. I made that choice to save us. With the money he's offering us, we can keep our heads above water for a few more *years* before we need to look someplace else. Think of that before you judge.'

Celine's jaw tightened, a muscle in her face feathering with the comment she undoubtedly swallowed so as not to throw it in her face. Restraint that Maria was grateful for. Though Celine was the child protégée, the eight years they had between them in age showed in situations like this, reminding Maria just how young her sister actually was and how her gifts had forced her to grow up far faster than any child should.

She glanced over at her niece, hoping that she could grow up at her own pace with the support of her mother and her aunt.

'You have feelings for this man, Maria,' Celine finally said, at which she instinctively scoffed.

'Feelings? Don't be absurd. This has never been more than a very innocent flirtation between two friends working together—taking the edge off the sometimes grim work we have to do.' Her chest tightened, and she prayed that it wasn't visible on her face. It was a small lie, one to comfort herself as well as Celine.

She didn't have *feelings* for Rafael, not the way her sister believed she had. Yes, she was attracted to him, and yes, the kiss they'd shared popped into her memory at the most inconvenient times, cascading sparks through her body that she willed away whenever they appeared. But this was all temporary. It would go away, she knew that, because there simply wasn't an alternative.

He didn't *want* what she wanted—and she didn't want him because of that.

'Oh, okay… If you believe that then I guess Darius and I will be ready for our couple's vacation once you come around.' Her sister's sarcasm bit, and Maria reminded herself that she was speaking from a place of hurt that came from the exposed wound of her estranged husband—Darius.

She needed to be patient as she introduced her to this temporary new reality.

'This is controversial, I get it. But I need you to support me regardless of your feelings. I made the choice, so we can only move forward from this point.' There were still a few open questions to discuss before they could move on from this.

From the scowl on Celine's face she could tell her sister was processing the information with sceptical reluctance as she asked, 'So how does this all work?'

Maria huffed a laugh at her directness. It was always straight to the point with her. 'We have to sell this marriage as real or his family could contest the trust and he wouldn't get the money.'

'What does that mean?' Celine asked, giving voice to the difficult question Maria had been rolling around in her mind ever since they'd got back from Manaus.

'I don't know... I'm not telling anyone that we're married. Otherwise, I'd also have to explain getting divorced so soon after. But outside of this house we'll have to pretend to... be dating?' Her voice rose to a questioning pitch, as she herself wasn't sure this was a sound idea. Only problem was—there wasn't an alternative. They *had* to at least show some level of affection whenever they went outside.

'Why do you need to pretend?'

'Because...' Maria paused and downed the remaining coffee from her mug. 'His family is trouble. I don't want to say much else because it's not my place. He's dealing with some messed-up stuff there, and that's a large part of why he chose to live here in the middle of nowhere.'

Though the sisters normally shared everything, it didn't seem right to share his story when it had taken him so much effort to confide in her alone.

Celine shook her head, crossing her arms. 'Maria, I don't know about this.'

'Remember when we found out you were pregnant? I needed some space to process my feelings, but I did that while we attended birthing classes together, read all the parenting books the library had to offer and turned our study into a nursery.' She paused when her sister's eyes narrowed. She knew where she was going with this. 'I need you to be like this now, okay? Process whatever you need to process about my fake marriage. But while you do that, I need you to support me.'

Celine took a deep breath, and Maria could almost feel the resistance to this idea. She was stubborn, all right. Most of the time that energy could be harnessed for great success, but the flipside was situations like this where she needed her to go along with something.

'What are you going to tell the kids?'

Another question Maria had been agonising over, and the obvious answer would get her another look from her sister. 'Honestly? I think we can just let them believe Rafael and I are dating. Nina is too young to understand the concept, and Mirabel… I'll explain to her that things didn't work out between Rafael and me when the time comes.'

A frown appeared on Celine's face. 'I don't like this,' she mumbled.

A buzz of the intercom at the wall interrupted the conversation, and Maria got up with a sigh of relief to check the little screen on it. Before she pressed the button, she looked at her sister over her shoulder. 'You don't have to like this. I just need you to play along until *our* charity is safe.'

She turned back around to press the button on the little screen.

'Yes, hello, how can I help?' she asked through the intercom as she studied the fair-haired man standing in front of the clinic's door. Her eyes narrowed on the pet carrier she spotted at his side. His face wasn't a familiar one.

'I'm looking to schedule an appointment with Dr Pedro. Is he here?' the man asked, looking up at the building as if he was trying to spot her.

Maria's eyes darted to her sister, who glared

at her in return. His name was the last one she wanted to hear from anyone right now.

'I'll be out in a moment,' she said into the intercom, then turned to go upstairs to put on something slightly less revealing than her PJs, pausing at his door.

Should she tell him someone was looking for him? She didn't recognise the person standing outside, and that was unusual in this small community. Maria shook her head, then stepped into her own room to get dressed.

She would handle the situation herself. If it was someone asking strange questions, she would be able to play the part of his doting wife. And if someone needed medical attention for their animal she could deal with that as well.

If the person turned out to be suspicious, she would tell him. If not, he didn't need to know. The last thing she wanted was to worry him unnecessarily.

Though it was Saturday, and technically his day off, Rafael found his way into the clinic in the late afternoon. A glance outside the window told him that Celine was out working, though when he came downstairs he only found Mirabel and Nina in the living room, with no trace of Maria. They informed him that she was in the clinic.

Restlessness sat deep in his bones and the one thing he knew to do was to dive into work headfirst to forget the warm tendrils of desire rising within him the more time he spent with Maria. A desire he didn't dare to utter, even in his thoughts, for the fear that he might ruin their friendship.

Because he knew he *didn't* want her to be more than his friend, not really. This feeling in his chest was nothing but an overreaction of his brain because their relationship had changed. Outside of the kiss they'd shared, nothing had happened that would change their feelings for each other, and even that kiss had been as fake as their marriage was. It had happened as a cover, in case his family had their spies inside the courthouse already. An unlikely scenario, but Rafael wasn't taking any risks when it came to his deranged family and their obsession with his money. Not after what they'd done with Laura.

A part of him was suspicious that his family hadn't made a move yet, hadn't even tried to contact him. What were they waiting for? It had been two weeks since they'd returned from their *elopement*, and his phone had stayed quiet. He'd expected them to try to get in touch with Maria, attempt to convince her that she didn't know him at all—that they were the victims in all of this, and Rafael was standing in the way of their dreams, that he had so much while needing so little. They knew he would never listen to them, so the only way they could get to him was to turn the people he cared about against him.

Just like they had done before with Laura.

Had they given up? That was too good to be true.

The door was unlocked when he pushed it open and he couldn't stop the smile from spreading over his lips. He'd worked in a lot of different clinics over the years, but none of them had been like this one. The intrinsic trust and affection people shared with each other in this town was so deep and warm. Rafael hadn't realised he'd wanted something like that his entire life. Someone like Maria, but also a place like Santarém where people were checking in on each other to make sure they had everything they needed—not because they were envious of their neighbours.

The thought of leaving it all behind broke his heart in two and only because he was giving it all up for the greater good kept him from hurting beyond repair. What he was doing—it was what the people of this village would do for each other without hesitation.

His ears pricked up when a soft rustling came from the area where they kept the animals for observation or post-op care. The thought of seeing Maria was as tempting as it was daunting. Since they'd come back, the energy between them had changed. They didn't run into each other as much, their morning coffee breaks invaded by this undercurrent of desire that threw both of them off.

There was no denying what was happening between them, or what they wanted to do about it. Nothing. Because they understood that they didn't have a future together. Because he cared for Maria, because she was his friend, he couldn't let her hang on to him for too long. He knew she wanted more from a relationship—true love. He wanted her to have that, and it hurt more than he was prepared to admit that he wasn't, and couldn't be, that person for her.

'Hey, Ma—' The words got stuck in his throat as she jumped out of her chair, clutching the baby ocelot to her chest while pointing the feeding bottle at him.

She relaxed when she realised it was him. 'Oh, my goodness, you scared me. What are you doing here?'

'What are *you* doing here?' he asked her instead.

'Me? Rafael, this is *my* clinic.'

He laughed at that, pulling up a chair from the other side of the room and sitting next to her.

'You could have asked me to take care of the ocelot if you want to hang out with the kids.' Even though he knew that this building and helping these animals was her entire life—and the reason she had agreed to marry him—he wasn't someone who just left after he'd seen his last patient, letting her deal with all the administrative stuff of the clinic herself.

Judging by the sparkle in her eyes, she recognised the efforts he'd put into this place as well, a grateful smile curling her lips.

'They know to come over here if they need any help. Plus, I didn't want to bother you on the weekend.'

'When your vet clinic is ten metres from your home, "weekend" becomes a very loose term,' Rafael replied, and the laugh he earned for it was so rich and vibrant that it made the hair on his arms stand on edge.

'Okay, but what are you doing here right now?' She looked around at the animals, searching for the one patient he might have come here to check on.

'I just needed to stretch my legs for a bit and so I thought I'd check in on some of our patients,' he said, leaving out the part where he was hoping to find her here.

'Lia here is doing a lot better. I think we can fly her to the institute soon.' She smiled at the little ocelot as she fed it.

'Ah, did you finally settle on a name for her?' he asked with a chuckle as he watched her press her mouth against the nozzle of the bottle.

'Mirabel did. I took her to see her a few days ago and she said she looked like a Lia.' Maria shrugged. 'I agree. It just seems right.'

'Do you have to take her to Manaus?' he asked, reaching out across the space between them to run his hand along the ocelot's back.

Maria shook her head. 'I know a shipping agency that has experience with exotic animals, so I don't have to take her. But she must go to the institute. With her being so young I don't think she could survive on her own just yet, and we don't have a way of tracking down her mother or anything. I'm not sure she'll ever be able to live in the wild now, but the institute is her best chance at that. They have some ocelots there that they're currently rehabilitating. If one of them adopts her as their own, we might stand a chance of getting her back out there.' Maria looked down and the gentleness radiating from her smile was so bright and pure that his breath caught in his throat.

It was moments like this that made it so hard to remember why he didn't want her in his life as his wife for the rest of eternity. In his mind he knew it wasn't about her, that it didn't matter who she was or how much time he actually wanted to spend with her. How he noticed every moment that he wasn't here, in her presence. That he wanted to learn from her, absorb her knowledge and her talent. Be blessed by her kindness.

But there was no way this could ever become a reality. He was too broken, his family too toxic to put anyone through it when he knew exactly how this would end. They hadn't shied away from infiltrating his life—his *heart*—to get what they wanted. They would not stop at genuine love either. No, they would somehow find a way into his inner sanctum and rob him of whatever little joy he'd been able to amass while they weren't looking.

If they ever found out that Rafael might harbour genuine feelings for Maria, they would use that as a weapon against him. Over the years in the entertainment industry, they had honed the craft of manipulating people—him included. He could not let them come here and ruin the goodness of Maria, of the people here in Santarém that he'd become so close to. Just by being related to them, he himself became tainted. He had already risked too much by getting attached the way he had.

As soon as matters were settled, he needed to leave.

'Let's hope for the best for the little one,' he said when he still felt her eyes on him, waiting for an answer.

'I want to shoot a small video with her before we send her off. They are organising a charity event to drum up funding for their newest project, and my colleague managed to get a slot for me in the presentation. Lia is the perfect subject to showcase what the charity is all about. Hopefully, she will catch the attention of a wealthy donor to help us out in the future.'

The prospect of Maria finding a new benefactor for her charity so soon struck unexpected fear in his heart, for he hadn't yet fully processed what would happen once their ruse was done.

He would have to leave, or he'd risk his family accosting her for the money they might think she possessed—or, worse yet, turn her against him. Even though the thought of leaving Maria and Santarém behind seared through his chest in a painful stab that forced all the air out of his lungs.

'I'm rooting for you,' was all he managed to press out, hoping that she didn't sense the inner turmoil their brief conversation had stirred up.

Maria remained quiet for a moment, looking down at Lia the ocelot, who wasn't showing any interest in her food any more. She got up in a fluid motion that had him run his eyes over her in an instinct to imprint everything about her into his memory, wanting to remember these precious few weeks he had spent here, enjoying his job and his place in life for the first time in years.

Who wouldn't with a person like that?

He followed her with his gaze as she put the ocelot back in its enclosure. Unlike during the week, she wasn't wearing scrubs right now but rather her casual clothes—if that wrap dress clinging to her curves could even be called casual. Even though the dress flowed at the back and around her arms, it sat tightly around her waist and chest, accentuating the beauty of her full Latina figure, and desire thundered through him with such a force that it knocked the wind out of him.

God, she was beautiful. How could he be

fake married to this person? How was it even possible that there wasn't an entire line of men waiting to court her?

The heat pooling in her belly ever since Rafael and she had started talking spread through her body in a star shape after she put down Lia and turned around, finding the man's eyes trained on her. The hazel colour of his eyes had darkened, his pupils dilated, giving voice and shape to the desire that uncoiled from the depths of her being. She breathed out with a slight tremble, the fabric of her dress rustling as she walked back to her seat, her skin alight with tiny fires that had erupted just below the surface.

Why was he looking at her like that—like the attraction between them was more than just an idle fantasy she liked to indulge herself in when her days got quiet? Because that was all there was to it, all there would ever be to this faux marriage. And the twinge this caused inside her chest could not be one of regret, because that would mean he meant something more to her than just a friend would—that just couldn't happen. Not with how definitive his answer had been around having a real marriage. Not with Mirabel living with her, who needed stability more than anything else. Her own needs hardly mattered when she weighed it against what her family needed.

And her family needed the doors to this clinic to stay open, to continue the legacy so many had given so much of themselves to.

'Anyway,' she said as she sat back down, her voice a lot lower than she had intended it to be. 'The reason I bring it up is that I would love for you to be a part of the video. You were the one who treated Lia, and I thought…maybe if they see us as a…family they will be more inclined to donate. I already asked Celine to take some shots of the market tomorrow, so we can sprinkle those in there along with Lia's story. It would be good if we can be seen there as well…together.'

The lump in her throat got thicker as she spoke, with Rafael's eyes still lingering, his arresting face schooled in an expression that made her knees weak. She watched as the same thoughts she'd had earlier rippled in different expressions over his face. Appearing together in public would put their ruse on display for everyone in the village to see. They'd have to convince everyone that they were a couple in love. Even if they weren't considered affectionate people, they wouldn't be able to keep their distance.

And, even though she didn't want to admit

it, the yearning for his closeness had driven her to extend this invitation more than anything else. Even if it was just once, Maria wanted to live the fantasy haunting her in her sleep.

'You want to spend tomorrow morning the way we usually do, but with a camera? Appear at tomorrow's market as a couple?' he asked, and if she had found her voice low, his was several octaves deeper, and ringing through her blood.

She swallowed visibly but nodded.

'If you want to capitalise on us being what looks like a family in the video, and this video will be shared with a wider audience, I hope you realise that we *will* have to ensure people believe we're a real couple. Depending on the audience the institute invite, some of my family's friends could be there. Chances are they will see this video. We can't give them any reason to doubt us if they see it, or they could contest the trust and draw everything out. I'm willing to risk it for you, but I need you to be aware of what you are asking me to do.'

A shiver clawed its way down her spine and she had to fight the urge to shake, even though she was pretty sure that he'd noticed anyway. Maria had thought of that, and the reward must outweigh the risk. The attraction between them was genuine, after all, their close friendship helping to show that they cared for one another. They would behave like a couple in front of the entire village, and hope that what they felt for one another was enough to pass scrutiny.

The thought of walking around town holding Rafael's hand sent a thrill of excitement through her that she fought back down into her subconscious. When had the desire between them escalated? A few weeks back, this had been no more than some smiles exchanged across the exam room, and now she was dreaming about the lips that had kissed her so gently. Imagining what they'd feel like on other parts of her body...

'Yes, I'm aware of that,' she said with another swallow, her heart slamming against her ribcage in an erratic dance.

Rafael leaned forward, the dark brown hair swaying over his brow as he braced his forearms on his thighs and looked at her—his gaze striking, stripping her bare without even touching her.

He got off the chair, the muscles under his shirt rippling with power and the promise of something primal that made her mouth go dry. Her breath trembled when he took a step towards her and her pulse ratcheted up with each subsequent step that brought him closer to her, until she needed to lean back to look up to him.

'Here's the thing, Maria,' he said, every note in his voice seeping in through the pores in her skin and sinking down into her body, every vibration of his rich baritone settling in a fiery pinch right behind her navel. His head dipped lower, his breath grazing her already heated cheeks.

'If we show ourselves out and about here in Santarém, we must pretend to be a real couple whenever there are people around us. This wasn't a problem when we went to Manaus to get married, because we were mostly alone. This will not be the same, even at a small market like ours. People *will* talk, and you know gossip can spread over several towns.'

Maria took a deep breath, not backing down from the intensity of his stare. 'I'm aware of that too.'

He leaned further in, his face going past hers and down to her ear, where he whispered, 'I don't know if I can stop pretending once we're behind closed doors again. It's already so difficult not to touch you.'

His voice was almost a growl as she turned her head to look at him again, seeing the fire raging within her stomach reflected in his eyes, the desire she'd convinced herself had been a figment of her imagination blazing in them—along with a promise of pleasure that had her curling her toes in her shoes.

'I might not want you to stop pretending.'

Rafael's mouth twitched, the corners of his lips quirking as if he couldn't believe she had just said that. Hell, she couldn't believe she had just said that either. Not once in her life had she been so brazen, no man ever catching enough of her attention to be worth stopping for him. Other things had always taken precedent—her studies, her career, her family.

And even this thing between them had only happened because she was trying to save her family's legacy, no matter the cost. But, in the process, this had also turned into something for her. A tentative permission to forget about caution, to give in to that tiny spark that glowed with delight inside her chest every time Rafael looked at her.

Even if this wasn't real, what if they pretended just for a few hours that it was? What was the worst that could happen? They both knew where this would end, knew where they'd get off the ride. So maybe she could let herself sink just a bit deeper into this thing with Rafael.

Rafael's hand came up to her face, but

stopped just shy of touching her, leaving a phantom of his touch on her skin that exploded a yearning for more through her body. 'Maria, I don't know if this is a good idea. What if—'

The rest of his sentence got cut off when Maria stood up, diminishing the space between them to virtually nothing, and then snaked an arm around his neck to pull him closer, sliding her lips over his in a kiss that she'd been longing for since his mouth brushed so gently over her cheek in Manaus two weeks ago.

Fourteen days of pent-up desire and sexually charged energy that culminated in this one kiss she pressed on his lips.

Rafael tensed for a moment as her hand came to a rest on his broad chest, and she thought he would pull away, that she had somehow managed to misread the signs of mutual attraction arcing between them since the day he'd started at her clinic.

But then he relaxed, his arms coming around her waist and his hands roaming up her back to press her closer to him in a crushing hug that confirmed what she hardly dared to believe to be true—that he was feeling this too and, more importantly, that he *wanted* this as well.

The kiss was almost the polar opposite of

the kiss in the courthouse. Where their first kiss had been tentative and shy, a mere whisper of the attraction between them, nothing more than a piece of performative art as they began their journey as a fake couple, this one was all tongue and teeth and weeks of repressed desire bubbling to the surface in an explosion of passion that had them both catching their breath.

Maria moaned against his lips when he slid his hands through her hair, pulling her head back to deepen the kiss. Her fingers roamed over his back, searching for anything to hold on to as her mind was set adrift with the onslaught of sensation, each part of her body reacting to everything that was Rafael.

Everything she'd wanted to have for the last three and a half months. How could she have ever doubted that she was making this up in her head? That being around him would ever be enough without possessing a piece of him that was only hers?

She gasped when his mouth left hers, the brief emptiness she felt there soon replaced with the kisses he lavished on her skin, making his way down to her neck and licking along the column of her throat in a primal, possessive move that had her knees trembling.

The sound of the animals around them

drifted to the back of her mind, leaving every one of her senses focused on Rafael and the fire that his touch left in its wake, each part of her body pliant and ready to submit to the desire that had finally escaped its tight cage.

Kissing Maria was better than he remembered—and so much better than he'd ever thought it could be. Though the kiss at the courthouse had everything to do with why he was here now, kissing her like the essence of life lay on her lips and he was all but one breath away from fading away, he'd sworn it was only for performance. That this would never happen again—could not happen again.

Because giving in to his desire for her was selfish. It was what he wanted with every fibre of his being, but from speaking to her he knew that this was not what she wanted. No, she wanted the fairy tale romance, a man who would bring joy and sunshine into her life— not one who was plagued with darkness the way he was.

He was being *so* selfish.

The thought barely managed to surface in his consciousness as his lips trailed down her neck, his nose nestling below her collar and breathing in her scent. She smelled divine, like the rainforest, sweet and earthy.

The strangled gasps dropping from her lips as his hand slipped up her thighs to caress her butt made Rafael hard, the ache originating from his chest extending through the rest of his body. He wanted to have her so badly, wanted to be the kind of person she needed in her life.

'Stop,' Maria said, and every muscle in his body went rigid at that command.

He withdrew from her a moment later, the clouds of passion filling his mind receding as he leaned back, chest still heaving from what had just happened. Maria was in a similar state, her breath leaving her nose in strained huffs that spoke of the desire he felt mirrored in his own body.

She looked straight at him, her eyes dark and filled with longing, bringing the already heated blood in his body to a near boil.

'Are we doing this tomorrow?' she asked, and Rafael had to take several breaths as his mind tried to catch up.

'What?'

'I need to know if you want to come with me. Be a part of the video,' Maria said, seemingly picking up their conversation where they'd left it before control had fully slipped Rafael's grasp and he'd given in to the need that had been bubbling in him since he'd arrived here.

'I… Did I just zone out for a moment and the last ten minutes didn't happen?' He looked down at her face, his eyes catching on her full dark lips, still swollen from their no-holds-barred kiss.

Maria seemed to notice his eyes drifting downward for her hand came up to her mouth, as if she also needed to confirm the phantom of his kiss still lingering there.

'I have two nieces, a sister and a fake husband who live with me. So I'm not exactly… available to do as I please right now,' she said in a low tone, each word chosen with such deliberation as if she was rethinking them as she spoke. 'But tomorrow the kids are at sleepovers and Celine is working. So… I will have the house to myself. *Ourselves*.'

Rafael paused, his brain still wholly focused on her full lips and the blood pooling in his lower body that it took him a moment to catch up. 'Oh… Oh.'

Maria had thought enough about him to devise this plan when an opportunity arose—both professionally, with the idea of the video, and arranging for them to be alone.

That thought should have struck terror in his heart, because it sounded like so much more commitment than he could give. She had made a plan with him. Plans. Those were for available people, not him, who had to look over his shoulder every waking hour of the day, who had moved into the heart of the rainforest to be as far away from his family and their drama as he possibly could.

Here, he had found his community and a woman who completely took his breath away, and she was now offering something he'd been dreaming about since his lips had first touched hers. The culmination of all their secret looks, sly touches and the ruse they had devised to save her business from ruin.

Rafael knew the wise thing to do here would be to decline, keep his distance and leave as soon as he transferred the money over to her. A smart man would do exactly that. Hell, he should probably already be interviewing for new positions, not lusting over a woman he knew he couldn't have.

Yet everything about her just made him want to yield. Yield to her talent, her compassion, to her stunning beauty.

'Nothing about our situation has changed, Maria,' he forced himself to say, his voice betraying the huskiness their kiss had stirred inside him.

He watched her carefully, looking for any

sign that she, too, had grown too attached. Did this invitation mean she wanted more from him, felt a similar yearning in her own chest? But her expression didn't alter, the only sign of nervousness her hands as she intertwined her fingers.

'I don't mean to change our relationship or the terms of our agreement. You have shown incredible generosity towards me and the animals we care for. Far more than I could ask for,' she said with a steady voice that didn't quite reflect what they had just done. 'This... invitation is something that exists outside of that. Something that has nothing to do with our deal and won't interfere with our plans.'

She dropped her eyes to her hands for a moment, then raised them again, the intense fire of passion in them inflaming his own need to be with this woman. He couldn't stop himself from leaning in, his head tilting back down towards her until their noses rubbed against each other. Then his lips brushed over hers in a tentative kiss, more exploring than passionate, as if to gauge her reaction.

Did she guess he planned to leave once the money arrived? Was that why she'd suggested what sounded like casual sex to act out what both had fantasised about for the last few months?

And he was leaving, so what was the harm?

'As long as we're clear that this isn't going to become anything more,' he said, and pulled her into another kiss, his tongue darting over her closed lips as if to underline his words.

'Crystal-clear,' she mumbled against his lips, and that was enough for Rafael to let go of his restraint once more.

His hand slipped along her spine and down to the small of her back, pressing her closer to him as his mouth claimed hers once more, putting all the desire and unfulfilled longing into this one kiss in the hope that it would serve to take the edge off...whatever this was that he felt for her. This unrelenting need to just *be* around her.

When Maria separated their lips with another huff that spoke of the fire burning within her—burning for *him*—he fully let go of her and stood up to bring some distance between them. If he let himself sink back into that kiss, he knew he wouldn't stop until they were both spent right here on the floor of her beloved clinic. Not the place he'd imagined when he'd thought about sleeping with her.

And he'd thought about that far more than he cared to admit.

'So tomorrow at the usual time?' he asked, his voice dropping by an octave.

'Yes,' she said, and he noted with a strange male satisfaction that this time her voice did waver, as if their kiss had left her rattled.

It certainly had left him catching his breath.

'I'd better go before I…' He left the sentence hanging in the air when the words eluded him. Before he dragged her down on the floor and made her scream with pleasure?

Even though they had agreed to do just that, it felt strange to say it so openly when most of their attraction had been conveyed non-verbally until now. Something he realised now that he had quite enjoyed, not wanting to spoil those moments with unnecessary words.

'I'll see you tomorrow,' she said with a smile that almost made him turn back to make good on the fantasy of having her right now, and he forced himself, with the last shreds of his willpower, to leave, having done none of the administrative work he'd planned on doing when he'd come here.

CHAPTER SEVEN

THE AIR BETWEEN Maria and Rafael was so thick she could almost grasp it with her bare hands. She wanted to blame it on the humidity of another midmorning in the rainforest rather than what lay between them. She had spent a restless night. Memories of their intense kiss had chased away worries about what to expect from today—what would happen tonight.

Celine had dragged her out of bed early so she could record a video of her feeding Lia. The way she had focused on her had Maria worried, but her sister guaranteed that it would be an eye-catching clip that would help them find a new donor.

Showing Maria and Rafael as a family had been her idea as well, which had surprised Maria. She'd come around to the idea of her fake marriage a lot faster than expected if she was already scheming on how to make the best out of this situation. Though she could see the value in it all—and at this point she was willing to try *anything* to find a new donor—the thought of being so openly affectionate with Rafael sent nervous flutters through her entire system.

What if they weren't convincing? Were they risking too much just to get some video footage of them holding hands while strolling through the town square?

Her stomach flipped over when Rafael reached out and placed his arm around her waist to pull her closer as they walked down the road to their destination. She looked up at him and saw none of the nervous energy fizzing within her reflected in his face. He'd slipped into the role of her husband without much effort—or was he just really good at hiding it?

'You look beautiful today,' he said with a smile that was so genuine that her breath caught in her throat.

Had anyone looked at her like that—ever? There was a nagging suspicion that she liked Rafael simply because he gave her the attention she had always rejected because she was waiting for *the one*—the person she wanted to make her family with. It was a thought so dear and intrinsic to her as a person that she had rejected casual dating or one-night stands, as she believed they would cheapen the connection she sought.

As the official head of their family charity she'd soon realised that she had to put everything she was and had into this to be successful. Her dream of finding the person to spend the rest of her life with would have to wait—or they would have to understand that helping these animals would be a big part of their shared lives.

Something Rafael definitely understood.

The thought scared her to her core, so she looked at him to distract herself. 'Thank you,' she replied with a small smile and leaned into his touch, wrapping her arm around him as well.

Hunger blazed in his dark eyes that tracked her every move as she swallowed, the same need setting her blood alight. Anticipation mingled with an unnamed fear of what they had promised each other for tonight.

They would play the part of the newlywed couple for the entire village to see. A risk that they had to take if they wanted to get the most attention in what little time the institute had been able to give her. With such a large audience of wealthy benefactors attending their event, she absolutely needed to go above and beyond to catch people's attention.

If that meant pretending in front of everyone that they were in love, then so be it. It was an act that came to her easier and easier as time passed, as if she was absorbing the role into her flesh and simply living it. Though she knew that wasn't an option—Rafael had said so on more than one occasion.

And while the unbridled desire she saw written in his eyes made her wet in anticipation, it also caused her heart to beat faster for him. How was she supposed to stop that when the fate of her charity was tied to this man and her pretending to be in love with him?

The mumbling of a gathered crowd drifted towards their ears and when they rounded the corner they saw a small collection of people milling around the town square.

'You ready for this?' he asked as he turned to her.

Maria nodded, parting her lips to reply, but before she could do so Rafael stopped and leaned down. His hand slipped onto her cheek, pulling her up towards him as he brushed a short but indulgent kiss onto her lips that made the words die in her throat.

'You okay?' he asked as they approached the crowd.

She looked up to him, wondering if she could sense a different kind of tension rippling through her body. One that had nothing to do with sex, but something much more primal, much deeper. The kernel of a truth she would fight until the bitter end, because letting it take root meant she would be doomed.

'Yeah...' she breathed, then looked to the front as they stepped into the milling crowd.

Like every Sunday, different vendors—both local and from the surrounding villages—had gathered on Santarém's spacious town square to set up their stalls. Several vendors were showing off their fresh produce, homemade cosmetics, cakes, honey, and Maria spotted a new person who was selling her crochet blankets and other accessories.

On the other side of the vendors were food trucks with people already queueing to get their early lunch served.

And, weaving in and out of the crowd, Maria spotted her sister, phone held out in front of her as she captured the entire scene. She paused in her tracks when she panned over to them, and Maria was suddenly hyper-aware of every single point where her body touched his.

Celine narrowed her eyes at them, then continued on her way.

'Well...she certainly can't wait to find a

new donor for us,' she mumbled, astonished at her sister's eagerness.

Rafael chuckled, and she was glad he wasn't taking Celine's behaviour as an insult. 'I don't see her here often. Or at all, really. Did you come here by yourself before I came along?'

Maria nodded. 'My parents used to bring us here every Sunday before they retired and moved to Switzerland. Celine stopped going shortly after. I always assumed it was because she was only doing it for them.'

'Why did your parents move so far away? Isn't Switzerland really cold most of the year?' He shuddered, drawing a laugh from her with his theatrics.

'It's a strange story, to be honest,' she said, turning around enough for his hand to slip off her waist. She reached out to grab his hand, then pointed at one of the coffee carts. 'Even though my mother loves all sorts of animals, she loves rabbits the most. So much that she developed a reputation as a rabbit special-ist throughout the country and people would bring their bunnies here for really complicated cases. Unfortunately, she was also *very* aller-gic to rabbits.

'But she didn't let herself be deterred by that, to the point where she had stressed her lungs so much with the exposure to them that she was left with respiratory problems. They always wanted to go and see Switzerland—it just seems like the polar opposite of what they had here. But when they realised how good the mountain air and low humidity was for her lungs, they decided to retire there.'

She paused when they got to the front of the queue to order their drinks.

Emanuel, the proprietor of the local café, started their order and heat rose to Maria's cheeks when he did a double take, his gaze dipping down to where their hands were intertwined.

'*Deus*, are you telling me that you two are finally…? Did you see Tina already? She is going to be over the moon to hear this,' the bearded man said, and Maria had to swallow the denial bubbling up in her throat.

She shot a sideways glance at Rafael, but if he was as panicked as her about the first comment about their fake relationship he didn't let it show. Instead, he smiled, raising her hand to his mouth and placing a gentle kiss on it.

'I knew the moment I arrived here,' he said with a smile so genuine that it took her breath away.

'People have been rooting for you two, you know that?' Emanuel said as he ground the coffee beans for their order. Years of experience meant that he didn't even have to look at his hands to know what he was doing.

'They have?' Maria's eyes went wide as the man nodded with eager excitement.

The *whole town* knew about her feelings for Rafael, and they were rooting for her? Had she really been that obvious? Sweat began coating her hand as the nervous energy around their outing today burst free from its restraints.

Rafael wrapped his hand around hers a bit tighter, shooting her a soft smile that mixed with the unease rising within her, plunging her insides into even more chaos.

'How is Rex? Did he recover from his food poisoning?' he asked to change the topic.

Rex was the dog they had treated some weeks ago when he ate some chocolate he wasn't supposed to. The man nodded with a grateful smile, the love for his pet obvious for everyone to see.

'He is much better, and now we have a new lock on the pantry so he won't be able to sneak in there,' he said, and handed over their coffee order to them. 'Seriously, please go find my wife and say hi. She's probably going to ask for a deposit for a wedding cake the moment she sees you.'

Maria swallowed as the words sunk in. They were acting like a couple, but the fact that they were actually married remained a secret. How would the people in the village react once they found out?

The nervous flutter in her stomach almost made her spill her coffee, her hand gripping Rafael's for support. He glanced at her, his expression one of calm and coolness and completely unlike the turmoil she was experiencing. Where were the nerves of steel she had honed through so many emergency situations when she desperately needed them?

She didn't have any time to further contemplate, for when they turned around to leave the coffee cart a trio of old ladies stood in front of them like a panel of judges—which was quite the apt description for them as they often served as Maria's judges whenever they put on a silly animal show for the village pets.

'*Bom dia, senhoras,*' Rafael greeted them with a smile so dazzling, all the women—Maria included—swooned at the sight.

'Well, if it isn't Santarém's most eligible bachelorette and her new squeeze,' Angélica, the leader of the troop of old ladies, said with a smile on her face.

Maria blushed, visible enough it seemed, for the ladies giggled while shooting each other knowing glances. How fast had this news spread? Emanuel couldn't have worked that fast, they'd left his stand but a minute ago.

'We're—' she began, but was interrupted by Lucinda waving a hand at her.

'Oh, you don't have to say anything, *querida*. We've known this was going to happen for quite some time. We're happy for you, right, ladies?' She looked around to her companions, who nodded eagerly.

'I mean… I might have been entertaining the thought myself for a while there. My dear José always said I should find love again. But I don't think he meant that to be while he was still alive,' Elisabete, the last one in the trio, quipped, and the other two laughed with her.

'If I run afoul of José, who will take care of my dry cleaning?' Rafael replied with an indulgent smile, at which Elisabete blushed.

Then he turned his gaze towards Maria, his hand releasing hers to snake around her waist and pulling her closer into his side.

'As it turns out, I found what I wanted right at home,' he said, and heat exploded through her entire body when he leaned in to feather a light kiss onto her temple.

The three *senhoras* sighed, giving him the reaction he'd undoubtedly wanted. Maria wasn't sure, for her brain had temporarily stalled as she processed what he'd said. He'd found what he wanted right here? Was he serious about that? No, he couldn't be. Falling in love was not a part of their agreement and whatever he said today wasn't real either. They were playing a role, and Rafael was simply better at it.

A thought that gave her pause. Either he was really good at pretending or she was terrible at seeing his behaviour for what it was—an act. Neither option boded well for her when she had invited Rafael to her place tonight because of what he'd said at the clinic yesterday—how hard it was for him *not* to touch her. Was that true or just part of the act?

They spent the next hour walking around the farmers' market the way they usually did, with only one key difference. Now people kept approaching them to express their happiness that they had finally become a couple—something Maria had been unprepared for. That meant that *everyone* had noticed her feelings for him develop. Everyone but her, apparently.

Rafael, meanwhile, gossiped and laughed with everyone who approached them, none of her own nervous energy showing in his interactions. It was the first time she noticed how seamlessly he'd integrated into the community of her tiny village. Everyone was just so…happy to see them together.

When they finally got to sit down with two plates from a new food truck claiming to sell authentic gyro wraps, Maria was too exhausted to dwell on what had just happened—how readily everyone had accepted their romance as genuine. This was something she needed to think about later, when she wasn't starving.

Celine sat two tables away with Nina and Mirabel, in an attempt to give them the privacy a newly formed couple might want from their first date in town. Maria's heart softened as she watched her two nieces share a slice of cake from Tina's stand while talking to each other animatedly enough that their voices drifted over to them.

'It's the first time I've seen Mirabel here at the market,' Rafael said when he noticed her gaze drift towards her family.

The smile that had just been pulling on her lips faded. 'She used to come here with her father. When he left, she didn't show any interest in joining us and I didn't want to force it on her…' she said, her voice trailing off at the thought of her brother.

Rafael's eyes narrowed, his expression turning thunderous at her words. 'He never asks about her? No calls or texts?'

She shook her head. 'No, he's not been in

touch since he left. We tried to contact him, wanted to arrange a truce, if only he would come back to see his daughter and be a part of her life again. Surely whatever this woman could offer him wasn't enough to abandon his child like that.'

Maria's hands curled into fists as she went on. 'I still can't believe my brother could do such a thing. I don't know what I would have done without Celine's help. We went through her pregnancy together, and I was the one who played the second parent role for Nina. So raising a child together isn't anything new for us…but, even then, we didn't know how we should…explain to Mirabel what happened. I mean, how do you explain that to a twelve-year-old?'

Her breath shook as she inhaled and a moment later Rafael's hand was wrapped around hers, leaving a sensation so warm and right she didn't want to imagine life without it. In moments like these she sought the comfort of a man's support, to help her through life just by standing by her side.

A dream that had lain dormant in her chest until Rafael had arrived in her life, sweeping her off her feet. Only what they had wasn't real either, no matter how she felt.

'What did your parents think about that? Did they ever come back to talk to him?'

Maria dropped her gaze down to her food, pulling at the soft pita bread without any intention of eating it. 'No,' she finally said as she looked back up. 'Celine and I debated whether to tell them, but in the end we didn't say a word about anything. They would upend their lives and come back here immediately. Neither of us want that for them, especially with how much our mother struggles with her asthma.'

'Mirabel's lucky to have you, you know that?' he said as he got up, circled around the table and sat down on the same bench as her so he could pull her into his arms.

'I'm not so sure about it,' she replied, letting insecurities she'd never shared with anyone bubble to the surface for him to see. 'I wasn't able to attract a new sponsor in time to keep the doors open.'

A gentle chuckle shook his chest, vibrating through Maria's bones as she remained pressed against him.

'But you did, just not in the traditional way you'd hoped to. You took on the burden to marry me and go along with my ruse to buy your charity more time. Not many people would be able to give so much of themselves to save their legacy.'

'Being married to you can hardly be called a burden.'

The words left her mouth before she could think better of them, flowing over her lips and into existence, sharing a piece of her that she had not intended to show him. Rafael stiffened under her hands, his muscles tensing in a foreboding way that struck dread in her heart.

Why had she said that? When she'd been the one to tell him that she would keep things separate, that their deal remained the same?

'What I mean—' she began to explain, but was interrupted by a familiar voice calling Rafael's name.

'Rafael, quickly!' Tina, Emanuel's wife and the baker of the village, urged when she came to a stop next to their table, her cheeks red and her chest heaving from exertion.

'What happened?' he asked as he and Maria jumped to their feet, a wary glance passing between them.

'I asked my daughter to bring some of the cardboard into the waste-disposal area. She asked me to come back with her when she heard a sound and we found something abandoned in a box.'

Her expression was distraught, telling Maria everything she needed to know. If Tina was

LUANA DaROSA

this concerned about the contents of a cardboard box, it could only be an abandoned animal.

The day had been the sweetest agony Rafael had ever put himself through. Being so close to Maria was intoxicating, every fibre of him that had been screaming for him to touch her as if she was his to touch finally satisfied as they'd walked around the town square.

Their outing had taken a sharp turn when they found a mother cat and her entire litter abandoned in a cardboard box among some other garbage. They'd rushed back to the clinic with their patients, and he was now examining the tortoiseshell cat with a soft and cautious grip.

'Who does something like that? Throwing away a cat and her babies as if they were no more than trash,' Maria said beside him.

When they'd tried to separate the kittens from their mother so they could give them a health check they had quickly realised that the cat was too nervous to be separated just yet. To avoid putting more stress on her, Maria had taken a step back and was observing and giving Rafael the space he needed to gain the cat's trust.

He sat down on a stool he'd pushed all the way to the exam table, remaining close enough to the cat for her to pick up his scent, but far enough so she wouldn't feel threatened.

'We don't know that someone dropped her off. This might be a stray that got comfortable in this box. From looking at her, she might have been there a day or two. She doesn't look malnourished, but she gave birth on her own without any supervision.' He glanced at the remnants of the cardboard box lying on the floor. 'They might have put her in there before she gave birth. Would explain the exhaustion I'm seeing in her.'

Her tortoiseshell pattern was a mixture of cream, dark brown and a blueish black splashed on her entire body in a chaotic pattern that was unique to this cat. His heart squeezed, both at the injustice of just being left in a cardboard box next to some rubbish, and also...

'She reminds me of my nanny's barn cat. It's the same cream colour, though the pattern was much different. I wonder if this one here is just as clingy as Donna. The moment I got on the farm, she wouldn't leave my side—would even try to climb into the car with me when it was time to leave.' He chuckled at the memory he'd long since forgotten. Even though his parents had been too busy chasing a dream that would never come true, his childhood had been more than that. He'd at least had Camila to look out for him, teach him about the farm animals and what his life could be if he applied himself.

'Does she have a chip?' Maria asked from behind him.

'I don't know.' He pushed the chair back and opened a drawer behind him, retrieving the scanner they used to scan the microchips some owners used for their pets. They contained important information about how to contact them in case their pet got lost.

He swiped the scanner over the cat to try to locate a chip, but the scanner didn't react—nor did the computer that would automatically search the country-wide database for a match.

'Doesn't look like it,' he said, putting the scanner down.

'Well…we can put her pictures up on our social media pages, but if no one claims her we can keep her and the babies until they are old enough to find new homes. Alexander won't mind.'

Rafael whirled around in his chair to look at her, his eyebrows raised. 'You would let me keep this cat in your house?'

The smile that spread over her face as he asked the question was so genuine and pure it took any remaining breath out of his lungs. He hadn't said much about the fond memories of his past, not much of the bitter ones either. Because opening up to her meant guiding her to a place he'd never shown anyone else in his life. But it seemed he didn't even have to open himself to her. Maria understood him intuitively, without any friction or tension. She knew when to stay close, when to let go and when to just be there.

How had he let this go so far? She was not meant to be this person for him who made his heart beat so much faster.

'Of course. This arrangement between us might be fake, but you're still my friend. You say you want to keep her, let's do it,' Maria replied.

And, just like that, his heart tumbled out of rhythm, leaving him with a cold sensation spreading through his chest. This was a gesture of friendship—what else could it have been? Despite acknowledging that friendship was all that had ever been discussed between them himself, he couldn't ignore the icy grip of disappointment.

'Let's see if we can find out more about her,' he said to turn the conversation in a different direction.

When he moved his hand to touch the cat

once more she twisted her head to look at him with bared teeth. Her ears were pressed flat to her head and a low hiss filled the air, making him take a step back to assess.

'She is too nervous for me to handle her. I don't know how long she's been in this box. She might be overstimulated and stressed.' He paused with a frown. 'I'd have to sedate her if we want to proceed.'

'Should I prepare some acepromazine?' Maria asked, getting to her feet.

Rafael looked the cat over once more, then shook his head. 'Without knowing anything else about her, acepromazine might already be too risky... Best to observe her for a few hours and then make a decision. Let's move her into a pen.'

Maria nodded, then opened a cupboard behind her and retrieved a bowl and a package of dried cat food.

'She must be hungry,' Maria said as she handed him the items.

Rafael poured the food into the bowl, then set it down in front of the cat. She sniffed at it for several moments, then with a shy and tentative bite took the offered food and chewed loudly on it before swallowing it.

'I'll go set up the pen,' Maria said, and left the exam room while Rafael stayed with the abandoned cat, observing her as she ate more of the food. When her ears popped back up and she no longer hissed when his hand came close to her, he felt confident enough to move her to the pen for observation.

Rafael was sitting in the back, watching the cat, when Maria stepped back in after checking in on some other patients that were staying with them. Instead of taking the seat next to him, she stood behind him so her stomach was touching his back and, in a far too intimate instinct, laid her hand on his shoulder. She breathed in his scent, the aroma of lavender calming her beating heart as she allowed herself this show of affection.

'How is she doing?' she asked as she watched him work.

'She's behaving fine. I don't see anything unusual. I think once she's had some time to recover we can give her an exam,' he said more to himself than to her as he cocked his head to one side.

Maria shifted her hand to lay more on his back as he bent down to look into the pen, and a moment later the door swung open. Celine stepped in, dressed in scrubs and the bag with all her equipment swung over her shoulder.

Her eyes rounded when she saw them, then

narrowed in an expression Maria knew meant
nothing good. They would have to talk about
this once they had a moment to themselves.

'I caught you finding the cats on camera.
Let me take some footage of her resting so that
I can include the happy ending as well. Pretend
like you are examining her.' She didn't wait for
them to say anything, but rather dropped her
bag on the floor and whipped out her phone.
Celine hovered over the cat and the kittens for
a few seconds, then she panned upwards and
urged Rafael to continue with his observation
with an impatient hand gesture.

Rafael furrowed his brow and glanced back
at Maria, who had lifted her hand off his back
but was still standing close enough to him to
feel his heat radiating into her. She gave a
small shrug.

'The kittens are eating well and she's no
longer reacting negatively to my presence.
Good sign. Means she is getting more comfortable,' he said, and shot a pointed look at
Celine.

'I got all I needed, thank you. I'll cut it all
together into a montage and upload it to the
website and our social pages.' She paused for
a moment, her eyes darting to the place where
Maria and Rafael touched, before coming back
up to look at her sister. 'You two be careful.'

She left and only those words remained hanging between them.

They stayed there for a while, watching the cat and her kittens settle in. When Rafael eventually turned to her his expression was veiled, but she sensed tension snap into place between them.

'Celine was right, you know. We need to be more careful, or next time it might not be your sister who walks in on us. What if we had said something about our arrangement?' His gaze was dark when he looked at her, genuine concern etched into his features.

'You think they would break into my clinic to talk you into giving them money?' Maria asked, scepticism lacing her voice.

'You don't know the things these people have done in order to get me to hand over my money to them,' he ground out between clenched teeth, sending a clear signal for her to tread lightly.

But his tone didn't stop Maria. They had shared enough closeness, enough passion and affection that she was done letting him shut her out. She raised her chin and squared her shoulders as she said, 'Then tell me.'

He opened his mouth but no words came out. Then Rafael reached around her waist, tucking her closer into a blissful embrace.

Maria's heart slammed against her sternum in an attempt to escape her body when Rafael pulled her into a hug that melted all the anxiety this day had summoned in her. All except one—and she was so certain that he wouldn't tell her about what had happened to him that she let her mind drift to what was waiting for her once they'd wrapped up here. Celine had left, taking the kids to their friends' house. It would be just them and...

Maybe this wasn't a good idea, after all. Though they had agreed that their desire for each other—and the decision to take their attraction to the final step—existed outside of their agreement, something inside her balked at the idea that he withheld so much of himself when she'd exposed so much more of herself than she had intended to.

Or was this the reason why she should be comfortable sleeping with him? Because, unlike her, he had not developed a deeper bond and didn't want to change their friendship. Otherwise, he'd have said something by now, no? Maybe he was saving them a lot of heartache down the line by keeping her at arm's length.

'I used to be engaged to a woman named Laura,' Rafael said, and she held her breath, not daring to say anything as he surprised her by replying.

'We were set up by a mutual friend, and I didn't think anything of it. At this point my parents had already tried to get me to marry the daughter of the CEO of another media company so they could benefit from this connection. Their hope was to combine resources so they could take advantage of his success.' He stopped, his chin coming to rest on top of her head, his heat sinking through the soft fabric of her dress and into her skin.

'I refused, like I refused many other matches they thrust my way, until they finally stopped bothering me. Though I should have known better, I thought I had refused them enough for them to give up. And then I met Laura, and it seemed to me that a lot of things in life suddenly made sense.'

Pain bloomed inside her chest as his voice revealed a hurt edge, mingled with regret. As if he lamented how things had ended between them. But how *had* it ended?

Maria didn't dare to ask, on the off-chance that it made him retreat again when he was finally sharing with her. So she let her hands roam over his back instead, each stroke calming and urging him to shed the defences she sensed around him.

'I fell for her in a matter of weeks—each time I met her bringing me closer to the conclusion that I had met my soulmate. The love of my life. For the first time, I thought maybe I could have this magical thing too. And so I asked her to marry me when we had our six-month anniversary. I had met the one person I was meant to spend the rest of my life with, so why wait, right?'

The hurt lacing his voice turned to bitterness, and Maria clung to him even harder, as if her touch could soothe the edge of those unwanted feelings resurfacing as he recalled those memories.

'One evening I dropped by my parents' house. Her car was in the driveway, which was strange because she knew how strained my relationship with them was. Still, back then I gave her the benefit of the doubt, thought she might have been there to mend fences. She had been urging me to bury the hatchet and, again, I didn't question it. Of course, she just wanted us all to be one happy family, the way we are taught to value family.'

He paused to let out a huff of contention. 'I got as far as the door before I heard Laura and my mother's raised voices filter through the open window.'

A small gasp escaped Maria's lips when

his grip around her tightened, his head above her moving. A moment later his soft breath grazed the crown of her head as his hands swept up and down her arms. The closeness they shared wrapped them in their own little bubble, tuning out the noise of the animals around them.

Rafael continued. 'My mother was asking Laura to convince me to move up the date of the wedding since they needed money right now. The idiot that I was, I still believed that my mother had lured her there under some false pretence, to pressure her in a way she knew she couldn't pressure me.

'But then Laura said it had taken her so much effort getting me to this point in the first place, she wasn't going to risk all of their payout just because my parents were getting impatient. "A few more months and then it's ours, and you'll get what you hired me to do." That was what she said.'

Maria's eyes went wide, her hand darting to her mouth, where she pressed it against her lips as the puzzle pieces regarding Rafael's stalwart defences fell into place. She couldn't help but raise her head to stare at him, her mind reeling from such a cruel betrayal.

'She…pretended to be in love with you for the money?' she finally asked when he remained quiet, his expression hewn out of stone.

'Since they hadn't been able to convince me to marry their choice of woman, they decided to sneak someone into my life instead. That was the moment I learned that I would never have love and marriage the way other people did, because the trust money would always ruin it. My parents, my siblings—their decisions were guided by profit, by what would help them succeed in this business they knew nothing about, so they could chase my grandparents' fame. And that was also the kind of people they attracted into their lives.' He shook his head, a rough, humourless laugh dropping from his lips that almost made her flinch in his arms.

'While my grandparents had the best intentions for us, they ended up cursing everyone with that clause in the trust fund. My siblings with unhappy marriages, and me to an eternity alone. Because of them, I will never know if someone is with me for myself or for the money they know I have waiting for me.'

'That can't be true. I—' She stopped herself from finishing that sentence when she realised where it was heading. Maria's interest in him, the connection that had formed way before they'd come up with their marriage ruse, had not been based on money but on genuine affection—on their friendship.

But how could she say that when she'd married him for the money as well? Was she any better than Laura, entering a fake marriage with him so she could save her own business?

Rafael shook his head, reading the thoughts reflected on her face. 'I entered this arrangement with my eyes wide open. Love was never part of the equation here, and we will separate with our dignity and hearts intact.'

Maria swallowed as doubt crept into her, its cold tendrils reaching across her body and settling in the pit of her stomach in an icy pool of blackness. Would her heart survive this, when it was already breaking for him?

She forced herself to nod, not feeling the confidence that gesture conveyed, and, by the look of scepticism on Rafael's face, he might not really believe her either.

'Thank you for listening to me. I've never told anyone this story,' he said, then he grabbed her hand and pressed it over his mouth, pressing a gentle kiss onto her palm.

A gesture that told her everything his words couldn't. That he wasn't scared she would break his heart like Laura had because, even though he liked and desired her, he would never love her. Would never let himself get so close to someone again because of what had happened to him.

And even though Maria knew that this should be a relief—because she didn't want to be with someone who didn't want the same out of life as her—a traitorous part of her heart broke off, shattering into tiny pieces as the far-fetched possibilities she had envisioned with Rafael scattered into the wind, along with the hope that maybe their connection was real, was more than just physical attraction.

Leaving her with a sense of sadness that she'd need to process once their divorce was through in a couple of months. But, until then, she would let herself have this one small piece of Rafael that he'd offered her and be glad of it, even if it wasn't what she truly wanted from him.

She could have tonight, at least.

So she swallowed the welling sensation of deep loss, locking it away inside her, and focused instead on what she knew he wanted of her—some physical closeness that existed outside and was removed from their fake marriage arrangement and her increasingly complicated feelings for this man.

'I think Mama and her babies are settled in. Do you want to get out of here?' she asked, and the dark gleam in his eyes as she said those words almost managed to push the doubts and longing for more away as he smiled at her, his face all male seduction and intensity.

'Let's.'

CHAPTER EIGHT

RAFAEL WAS IN deep trouble. He'd suspected that from the first moment he'd walked into Maria's clinic and been unable to take his eyes off her. And over the months they'd interacted with each other the innocent friendship that had clicked into place when they'd met had evolved into something more tangible, more real, that infused his blood with new life. But he knew that he'd made a mistake, let things grow too far, get too comfortable, when his lips brushed over hers in a gesture that could barely be described as a kiss.

The idea to get fake married had been necessary even though he'd known it would be a struggle for him to keep detached. He'd had no chance of doing that when he was already so invested in the fate of this town, who had given him a home when he'd needed one. When his own family had pushed him away with their actions...

He had long since made peace with the fact that he would never have access to his fortune and that he'd gladly trade it to have a life away from the toxicity that was his family. And then Maria had confessed to being in trouble, and he'd *needed* to help her, knowing he would regret not doing so more than the sacrifice he knew waited at the end of this arrangement for him—he needed to leave. Despite that, there'd been no way he could stand by when he'd held the solution.

Because he wanted her—so bad that it was hard to breathe, impossible to think straight, to…remember why they could never be together.

The tension between them finally snapped when they walked upstairs to the door Rafael had been staring at with hidden longing ever since he'd moved into her house. She stepped over the threshold of her room—right where he needed her to be, to give in to this fantasy he'd been nurturing in his heart for so long.

'So Raf—'

The moment the door closed behind them, Rafael turned around and grabbed her by the waist, hauling this woman into his arms, his mouth crashing down on hers. Urgency unlike any he'd ever felt before gripped him, his hands roaming over her body as the need to explore every inch erupted in him.

Maria went soft and pliant in his arms, leaning into the touch with a soft moan that rippled through him in a tidal wave of heat and ice, creating a storm in his chest that threatened to break loose and take him with it.

He wanted to pause, to go slow and savour every moment of this one night they had. Because one night was all they were going to get. One night to live like this thing between them was real. But the primal part of his brain had taken control of his body, urging him to let go of his final hesitation when the woman he cherished and longed for lay in his arms.

A deep peach colour dusted her high cheekbones as he pulled away from Maria to look at her. Her lips were parted in a soft sigh, her eyes ablaze with the same intensity rocking through his own body. His hand came to rest on her cheek, his thumb brushing over her heated skin.

'Sorry, I interrupted you. That was impolite,' he said, his voice all thunder and gravel with barely restrained need.

'I…' Maria blinked twice before a tentative smile spread across her lips. 'I don't think I remember what I wanted to say. This is better than talking anyway.'

Then she leaned forward, lush mouth pressing onto his as she gave him silent permission to continue, her eagerness such a turn-on that his blood rushed to the lower half of his body and he gave a muffled groan. His hand slipped into her hair, cradling the back of her head as he pulled her deeper into their kiss, his tongue sweeping over her lips and begging for entry.

Maria sighed into his mouth, a sound filled with longing and pleasure that set his entire skin ablaze. Then she opened her mouth to his tongue, and what he'd thought to be everything his body had to offer intensified again, bringing him to a higher plane of existence as she met his every stroke with the same urgency and need.

'*Deus*, Rafael…' she whispered when they broke apart, her chest heaving as she caught her breath.

He kissed her again, gentler this time, a mere brush on her passion-swollen lips, before he moved down to nuzzle her neck. The scent of earth and flowers filled his nose, sending a renewed wave of pleasure through his system as he breathed in again. He wanted to remember this scent for the rest of his life. It was the fragrance that drifted through the clinic whenever he arrived in the morning, mixing with the quiet longing that he had nurtured in his chest despite knowing better.

If this should be the one night they had with one another, he would make it count.

The world around Maria faded away as her senses homed in on Rafael and where their bodies touched. There was no bedroom around them, the soft carpet only a faint sensation as her toes curled into it. There was only him and the touch she'd hungered for since she had first admitted her attraction towards the new vet all these months ago.

Now his fingers were tracing down her side and with it soft trembles that left her mouth in shaky sighs. How was she going to survive this exquisite torture, where every touch, every breath grazing her skin hurt in the most pleasurable way?

His teeth scraped over the sensitive skin of her neck, his hands slipping lower and lower until they rested on her butt. The fabric of her summer dress rustled, the only sound in the room outside of her soft moans as Rafael explored her body at his leisure, seemingly in no hurry to get the clothes blocking them out of their way.

Rafael's hands slipped back up, trailing to the front of her body, where his fingertips grazed over her breasts as his mouth dipped further down to kiss her collarbone.

'Tell me what you want, *amor*,' he whispered against her skin as his hands moved further, settling right next to her zip.

He chuckled against her neck when she arched her back, pushing against him with her hips. 'You,' she replied, feeling his considerable length straining against her.

Deus, were they really going to do this? Unbridled need mingled with a low simmering panic at the prospect of sleeping with Rafael, letting him see her as hardly anyone had ever seen her. It had been years since her last time, so long that every touch had her sensitive and yearning for more.

But, instead of continuing downward, Rafael brought his face back up to hers, his nose gently stroking the side of her own. 'I want to know what you like, Maria,' he said before he kissed her again, her knees shaking from the unending gentleness of his kiss.

What she liked? That question had never factored into any intimate moment she'd had so far—which wasn't a lot to begin with. Had no one ever asked her this question before? She'd not been with a man in two years, and before that her relationships had been few and far between.

The fire in her dampened, making way for insecure confusion as her eyes slowly drifted back into focus. The extent of her inexperience had never bothered her…until now.

'I…don't know what I like,' she finally admitted, and had to swallow the sigh of relief building in her throat when Rafael only smiled at her, before coming back in to steal another kiss off her lips.

'Let's try a few things and see if you like them. But you have to tell me what works for you and what doesn't.' His voice was deep, filled with gravel and promise that by the end of this night she would *definitely* know what she liked.

That tone alone sent a shockwave through her that settled in an agonisingly needy pinch right in her core. A shudder trickled down her spine, shaking her every limb. Rafael must have felt it as well. His smile turned pure male when his fingers finally grabbed her zip and pulled it down, exposing the skin of her back to the cool room.

Another shiver shook her when he peeled the dress forward as she took out her arms. Another tug and the dress glided down her body, pooling around her legs like a flowery puddle of water. Rafael took a small step back, enough for him to see her without having to let go of her hips. The hiss he let out as his eyes roamed over her bare breasts and the small black lace triangle that covered her sent a hot spear of pleasure through her.

The reverence in his expression was something she had never seen before, cascading goosebumps all over her skin as his hands slid back up, gently caressing her ribs before they palmed each of her breasts with a gentle squeeze that shot fireworks into the pit of her stomach.

'Good thing I didn't know how exposed you were underneath that dress or I wouldn't have been able to play the dutiful husband for you all day,' he said with a grin that caused her breath to hitch as images of him dragging her into the clinic's broom cupboard to bend her over flashed through her brain, making her dig her toes into the plush carpet.

'You are just...*perfeita*,' he murmured.

Maria opened her lips to say something, but only a strangled moan came out when Rafael brushed his thumb over her erect nipple.

His breathing became just as laboured as hers when he did it again, watching another moan build in her throat as her eyes squeezed shut and her body twitched under his touch. Heat rose to her cheeks, her hands digging into his shirt as if that would help her to hang onto reality as the room around her grew even dimmer.

She thought she was getting used to his touch, her skin less sensitive, until he dropped his head even lower and took one of her dark brown, taut nipples into his mouth. The universe around Maria shattered into a million pieces which all drifted away into nothingness. There was only her body and his, each touch so intentional and aimed to please her.

It wasn't like anything she'd ever experienced.

'Is this good for you?' he asked as he pressed his lips against the skin between her breasts, each word forming a kiss on its own.

'Yes…' she replied, barely able to get the affirmation out as his lips wandered over the swell of her breasts to the other nipple, repeating the delicious process with cruel slowness that left her shaky on her feet.

Maria's hands were still grasping at his shirt, pulling him closer despite the lack of space left between them. With each lick of his tongue her mind had drifted further away, the overthinking and worry about their future or what this meant for their arrangement floating away. Her lack of experience was only a small noise in the symphony that was Rafael's touch.

Her body took over as the worry vanished

into nothingness, and her hands found the buttons on his shirt. Eyes still closed from the pleasure rippling through her, she felt down his chest, her fingers almost frantic in their quest to get rid of the fabric impeding her senses.

His lips vibrated as he chuckled again, teeth still scraping over her nipple as he rolled his tongue over it and sent a lightning bolt of tension and pleasure right to her core. The emptiness that followed when he let go of her was almost too much, and Maria instinctively pushed her chest out as if to reach for him.

'You want this gone?' Rafael grabbed both of her hands that were unbuttoning his shirt with a haste and greed that made his erection twitch in his pants.

Though he strained for release and wanted nothing more than to entangle himself in the bedsheets with her, he forced himself to take it slow. Though she hadn't said anything explicit, the way she touched him spoke of something so special and innocent he wanted to ensure that their night together would be exactly what *she* wanted and nothing else. That she couldn't tell him what she liked was an indication of how selfish her lovers in the past must have been.

A thought he pushed away as his temper surged at that. How could anyone look at this woman without giving in to the urge to worship her for however long she pleased? If she was willing, he would do exactly that, no matter how much he himself ached.

Her eyes were ablaze with a want that made him swallow hard as his breath came out in ragged bursts. 'I want all of it gone,' she said, confidence ringing in her voice for the first time since they'd started making out.

He shot her a grin, lowering his head as if to sketch a bow. 'Tonight, your wishes are my command, *amor*,' he said in a low rumble before he loosened the remaining buttons and shrugged the shirt off.

Then his hand went onto his waistband, but Maria's hands clasped around his wrists before he could do anything.

'Let me,' she said, causing another twitch of his manhood as he anticipated her touch with an unbridled eagerness that almost made him burst on the spot.

Taking a deep breath, he nodded and watched with narrowed eyes as she unbuttoned his trousers, revealing his erection straining against the fabric of his underwear. The last barrier that stood between them.

She stared for a moment, her lower lip vanishing between her teeth as she looked at him, his desire for her on display for her to judge. Of course he reacted instantly to her touch when he'd longed for her from a distance for so long—spending long nights in solitude with nothing but his thoughts and her lingering scent to keep him entertained.

Rafael had been lost from the start, enthralled by her dedication and love towards her animals and the lives she saved every day. Who could resist such a powerful and sensual woman?

His thoughts scattered when she reached out with two fingers, tracing the outline of his length against the dark fabric of his briefs, smiling when she got a longing twitch as a response to her touch, begging her for more of her, more of everything.

'*Deus*, Maria…' he gritted out, and the appreciative laugh he received in return nestled its way into his chest and settled there, soft and warm. 'I've wanted this for so long.'

She looked at him, her eyelids heavy with the desire zipping between them. Her palm grazed over him again as she brought it upwards, then she grabbed his hand and guided it towards her front, where the tantalising lacy thong still covered her. With a smile lighting up her face, she pressed his hand against herself as she whispered, 'Me too.'

Rafael swore under his breath as dampness clung to his fingers that had soaked through the fabric. He'd known she wanted him, otherwise she wouldn't have invited him to her room. Yet somehow the confirmation of it, feeling her eagerness for him loosened all the restraints he had imposed on himself.

Slowness suddenly seemed like an unnecessary torture he'd agreed to put himself through. He needed to hear her pleasure. Now, or he might explode from all the sensation rioting in his body.

As he captured her mouth once more, he worked the fingers she had just placed on the apex of her thighs in a slow circle through the almost sheer fabric. Maria's reaction was instantaneous. Her hips bucked forward as his passionate kiss swallowed the drawn-out moan escaping her throat. Her head lolled backwards as he continued, her breaths increasing as her lips parted.

Rafael watched her with intent, took note of every facial expression, every twitch of her mouth as he pushed her thong down and slipped his fingers through her folds.

'Is this what you want?' he whispered close to her ear, relishing the soft mewls that were increasing in volume with each stroke of his fingers.

'Yes, this is *exactly* what I want,' she huffed out between moans, her hands clawing at his back as if they were searching for anything to hang on to as he pleasured her. 'I'm so…close.'

The last word came out mingled with a sound of such guttural pleasure that his eyes fluttered shut as he reined in his own release barrelling towards him.

He hissed when he slipped a finger into her wet heat, the sensation so tight and perfect as she moved her hips against him.

'Do it for me, Maria,' he said against the shell of her ear, kissing her just below and down her neck as he increased the pressure of his fingers.

A blinding white light flooded Maria's senses as her mind got lost in the currents of her own pleasure, the warmth of her climax spreading through her as her muscles clenched and released.

It took her a few breaths to realise that the scream that had echoed through the room was her own. Her hand flew to her mouth as the realisation struck.

'Oh, my God,' she whispered behind her hand, shaking her head.

Her eyes widened as she met his gaze, pure and primal masculinity written in his eyes. The gleam of a predator that was studying his prey. The intensity sent renewed shivers through her body, disturbing the balance of already unsteady feet.

Her inner voice had long since quieted, letting her body do what it knew to do through instinct alone as she gave herself to Rafael and discarded the last vestiges of modesty to be with him. And now she really *needed* to be with him, for the fire burning inside her had not been extinguished but merely tempered by the aftershock of her orgasm. The way his dark gaze roamed over her reignited her core again, her body pliant and ready for his touch.

Without overthinking it, she slipped her fingers under the elastic of his briefs and tugged at them, bringing them to his ankles in one move. A sound loosened from his throat that sounded like a growl escaping from deep within him. She stripped off her own underwear and gave in to what her legs had been begging for several minutes now—she let herself fall backwards and onto the bed, arms propped up so she could look at him with passion-glazed eyes.

'I want you,' she said, her eyes pointedly

dropping to his erection, 'to do what you just did with your fingers.'

That was what he'd asked for, wasn't it—for her to tell him what she wanted? The idea had shocked her a few minutes ago, bringing forth a shyness she didn't know she possessed in the first place. Confidence was her default when she dealt with animals, nervous owners and anyone else bringing animals into her care. Maria had worked hard to become an authority in her field, to command legitimacy when it came to the effects of deforestation on the local wildlife.

Speaking to people was something she did every day, yet she froze when Rafael asked her what she wanted, unable to voice what was in her head. It was simple.

I want you.

The words echoed in her mind unspoken, knowing that she couldn't have that, couldn't have him be hers alone. Even voicing that desire would be a betrayal of their agreement. So, instead, she had to remember this night and everything it meant to her.

Rafael grinned at her request, then bent down to scoop up his trousers from the floor. His hand slipped into the pocket, and he held a small rectangular packet between his fingers when it reappeared.

An involuntary laugh left her lips when she recognised what it was. 'You were carrying a condom with you all day?'

He shrugged, ripping it open and rolling it down his shaft. When he turned back towards her intent gleamed in his eyes and Maria shuddered with anticipation.

'When I saw you in that sexy summer dress, I wasn't sure how fast we would get to the main event,' he said, then approached the bed and crawled over her, his body covering hers. 'You have been very hard to resist, as I'm sure you can tell.'

Maria gasped when his length came to rest between her thighs, excitement clenching her core.

'Kiss me,' she whispered back at him as she wrapped her legs around his waist, shifting him to where he needed to be.

Rafael brought their faces together. 'I can't tell you how much it turns me on when you tell me what you want.'

She didn't get a chance to reply, for Rafael closed the tiny gap between them and laid his mouth over hers just as he angled his hips towards her to push into her. Her moan was swallowed by the dance of their tongues moving against each other as he thrust in and out in a steady rhythm that spelled comfort and safety.

Understanding. That was what Rafael had brought into her life from the very beginning. A deep sense of understanding for her work, her passion, the predicament she had found herself in. He shared her ideals, loved working with animals just as much as she did, and throughout their fake marriage he'd not once made her feel like she was less to agree to such a deal in the first place.

Her hands clawed against his back, digging into the strong muscles there that bunched and released as Rafael kept their tempo, each thrust bringing her higher, to a place that was filled with pleasure and his scent that she couldn't get enough of.

'I'm almost there again. Please, Rafa—' she started, the rest of her words disappearing as her body trembled, bringing her closer to the edge again.

Rafael's elbows came down on each side of her face as he thrust deeper, his forehead touching hers, a primal grunt filling his throat as he forced a breath out of his chest.

'This is so much more than I thought it would be,' he whispered against her skin, just as the borders between pleasure and pain blurred for the second time today.

Maria's head fell back, her mouth open with another moan of pleasure as her muscles squeezed tight before releasing her into a blissful state of nothingness.

His words barely registered as he, too, let out a groan, his fists bunching into the sheet as they came together, leaving him trembling on his elbows until he gave in and collapsed on top of her.

Maria smiled through the bliss, her fingers running through his short hair and down his spine, picking up beads of sweat as they trailed over his back. This moment was perfection— but it led her to a realisation that she wasn't ready for, yet could no longer ignore as she had done over the last couple of weeks.

Rafael was who she wanted to be with, and as he looked at her with those passion-glazed eyes, seeing the respect and affection lying underneath, Maria felt her heart crack as she realised that she wouldn't be able to lose him—not without her heart fully breaking apart.

CHAPTER NINE

THE NIGHT AFTER they had played a married couple for the entire village, and the subsequent week, had been an out-of-body experience for Rafael in more ways than one. Though they had agreed that their night together would exist outside of anything else they had going on, neither of them were able to keep away from the other.

Hot kisses were stolen between patients, each one filled with a sense of urgency and longing that gave Rafael pause. He knew where this was coming from—the deadline was approaching its end.

After their first night together, Rafael's lawyer had informed them that the final paperwork was being processed by the bank and that they'd be able to release his funds in two weeks. Though neither was willing to spell it out, they treated each kiss as if it were the last. Because their breakup was inevitable—

and the devastation this thought summoned in him was one of genuine heartbreak.

Despite dismissing the risk of this happening as minuscule, Rafael had fallen for this amazing woman who had agreed to be his wife to save her family legacy. The people in his life had always been in pursuit of their own agenda, serving only themselves and their goals to the point where he'd believed all humans to be like that.

Until Maria had come into his life, and he'd suddenly understood what had been missing all those years filled with emptiness—her. And even though he recognised the kernel of light growing within his chest as genuine affection and love, he had to leave. He *had to*, because his family would never let him have this happiness. No, he was tainted by association alone, and because she and this place had become so important to him he needed to go. The curse his grandparents had created with their trust bound him to his family, not letting him lead a normal life. His bags were already packed with whatever he had left in his room, ready to leave this town—and the promises it held—behind, to vanish into obscurity.

It surprised him that his family hadn't made a move yet, that they hadn't heard about his marriage. Maybe they had believed Rafael when he had told them he would never get married, so they'd stopped keeping an eye on him. Though if they didn't pay attention now, they would when they heard that he had access to the money in his trust. He needed to be gone from here before they found out or they might find Maria—might learn how much she meant to him and use that against him.

As if his thoughts had summoned her, Maria opened the door to his small office, a wary expression on her face. His back stiffened at the alert in her eyes, and he whirled around in his chair.

'What happened, *amor*?' he asked, the endearment slipping out before he could help himself. Love. That was not what he should call her—ever.

'Celine sent me a picture of a headline in a magazine. She's on her way back here, but…'

Rafael's blood ran cold at her words. He got to his feet, his hand wrapping around her arm and pulling Maria closer. 'This must be my family's doing. I was wondering when they would get involved in our deal and try to give themselves a pay day from my money.'

He swore under his breath when he looked at a picture of them kissing, plastered on the front page of a minor tabloid in Brazil—a small blessing. Clearly the major publications weren't interested in the grandchild of former *novela* stars.

'Pedro Media's disgraced son seen with rural vet,' he read out loud, then sighed at his own description.

Disgraced son? That must have been his parents' idea, planting the rumours that he had run away and turned his back on the family business, when it had been their toxic behaviour that had forced him to make that decision. Family was everything in their culture and that they had told people he had gone without so much as a word or care brought a wave of nausea that rippled through his body. What if someone in Santarém read this and believed them over him?

'How did they get this picture?' Maria wondered.

He looked at her through narrowed eyes, taking in her expression. She sounded more curious than outraged. How could she not have an instant and visceral reaction to such a betrayal of their privacy?

Rafael looked at the picture, frowning. It showed them locked in an embrace here in the clinic. His family had sent people to check on him after all. He just hadn't seen them. Clicking on the photo, he found who the photo had originally belonged to before they'd licensed it to the publication. Then he showed Maria his screen with a picture of the photographer on it.

Her eyes widened in recognition.

'You've seen him around the property?' he asked, his voice sharp.

Maria nodded. 'He rang the doorbell some weeks back and asked to speak to you. You were still sleeping, so I went to see him. He… had a cat with him, so I didn't think anything of it when he asked for you. I didn't say anything because…he was just another patient.'

Colour drained out of her face. 'This man was stalking around my property with a camera and a cat as a *prop*? Where did he even get it from?'

Rafael stepped closer to her, his arm coming around her waist as if his embrace could protect her from the media circus his family was trying to inflict on them. This would be only the first step in many to wear them down, and he knew exactly what they wanted in return.

'I'm sorry you've had to find out first-hand how unhinged my family are. They will not stop until they have my money.' He paused, a lump appearing in his throat that he had to swallow before he could continue. 'It will only be a week or so until the transfer is through. Then I can make my donation and be on my way.'

'Wait… You're—'

The door swinging open interrupted Maria, and his arm tightened around her instinctively, hauling her closer to him. They both relaxed when Celine stared back at them. Her eyes darted down to where his hand clung to Maria's hip, then she shook her head.

Whatever communication had passed between them about his relationship with Maria must have been silent, for after a shake of her head Celine nodded towards the computer Rafael had been working on moments ago.

'Did you look at it?'

'Yes,' he said.

At the same time Maria breathed, 'No.'

They turned their heads towards each other. Rafael was the first one to speak. 'You didn't come here to show me the tabloid picture?'

'I did, though not because of the reasons you think I did,' Celine replied, then brought her phone back up to show him the article associated with the picture.

'The video I made last week for you to send to donors? I included the footage of us finding the abandoned cat. For reasons beyond me, this tabloid thought it was a good idea to embed the video in the article,' she continued as she sat at the desk to bring up the website of the animal charity.

'Wait, so they went to our social pages to include a video that's an ad for our organisation?' Maria asked, furrowing her brow.

'Yeah, no idea who came up with this. But… it worked out great for us.'

Rafael looked at Maria, who stared at the article on her phone in bewilderment. As she scrolled down, the video appeared. Lia immediately caught the attention of any viewer, and after the first two seconds Celine's voice started to narrate the benefits their charity brought to the community.

'I don't understand how this is good for us, Cee.'

Maria stepped closer to her sister to look over her shoulder as Celine explained. 'After Daniel left, we realised we wouldn't be able to keep ourselves afloat with the current donations, so we put a cry for help on the front page so anyone visiting it would know to donate. We put up a counter so people could see what impact their donations were making, however small.'

Rafael shot her a questioning look. 'You think enough people read this to have an impact on donations?'

Both sisters shook their heads. Then Celine said, 'No, but because they included our video, a famous animal rights activist saw our compilation and highlighted it on her own social media pages. She has over a million followers and chose to highlight our charity after watching our video and hearing our call for donations. That video—along with our own—got shared like crazy in the last week. It went absolutely viral.'

She stopped, looking at Maria. Both of their expressions were incredulous. The donation target on their website was set to five hundred thousand. A number next to it was blinking in a grass-green colour, and Rafael immediately understood why both were suddenly lost for words. The figure read three million.

'*Meu deus...*' Maria whispered, first looking at Celine and then at him. 'Can someone tell me that this is really happening?'

His heart squeezed tight at the unreserved happiness in her gaze as she smiled at him. 'This just bought us so much time,' she said, then jumped off her chair in a sudden move to hurl herself against Rafael.

Her hair obscured his face as he wrapped his arms around her midsection, drawn towards her for what he knew to be one of the last times. Though the relief in her voice touched something deep inside him that he didn't dare to examine closely for the fear that it would make him reckless, his chest tightened as the plans he had been stewing over for the last several days were set into motion.

'Listen, Maria…' he started, but got cut off by Celine.

'How many of them do you think are monthly donors?' she asked as she took a seat in front of the computer.

Maria twisted in his arms to look at her sister. 'We can check the registration forms.'

She moved out of his grasp but then briefly turned around again. 'What were you going to say?'

Rafael shook his head, not wanting to spoil the moment with news he knew would hang like a dark cloud between them. 'Nothing important. I'll talk to you in the evening.' He paused, then said to both sisters, 'Congratulations. I'm glad you get to fight for the animals that need you yet another day.'

Maria beamed at him, a look so filled with affection and warmth that he had to immediately turn away and leave the room. She could not look at him like that. Not when he was about to let her know that he would be gone tomorrow.

Sooner or later his family would find a way to ruin this relationship, to turn her against him. Or worse, they had their fingers in it all along. The way they had with Laura. Rafael wanted to preserve his memory of this place—and her memory of him—so even though the decision to leave had caused a constant pain in his chest, the choice remained the same.

Better leave now and preserve what they had built with his legacy than wait for his family to lie and manipulate their way into Santarém, into Maria's family, making him out to be the person who'd destroyed their family.

The day had gone by in a flash after the explosive news of the morning, with both Maria and her sister reeling at what had happened to them. Whenever she had thought of a new sponsor, she had always sought out people with big money. Never had the thought of approaching strangers on the internet crossed her mind—though now it seemed like that was what she should have done in the first place. That a clickbait article about his family's media company should be the thing that saved her family's legacy from complete ruin was too much for Maria.

Most of the donations were one-off gifts from sympathetic people who had seen the viral video of Rafael finding the cats in the box, but there were enough monthly donors to keep them operational. More would be better, but now that this had been revealed as an option Maria could spend more time finding the kind-hearted people who cared about animals just as much as she did rather than going after rich people who had too much money and not enough things to do with it.

It also meant that she didn't need Rafael's money any more. With the reason for their fake marriage gone, did they need to stay together?

It was that part that poured icy water through her veins, filling her with a sense of dread. Because this was always supposed to end. From the very beginning their fake relationship had an expiry date that they had agreed on. Was it disingenuous of Maria to want to change that? To give in to the real feelings this faux marriage had conjured up within her?

After the weeks they'd spent together, Maria had to admit to herself that she was in love with Rafael. Had been heading in that direction even before they had made this deal, when they were still trying to be friends.

Maria's head sank into her hands as she thought of the choice ahead of her, her chest squeezing so tight it became hard to breathe. A desire manifested within her, one so wild and outrageous that she couldn't believe it was even living inside her mind.

She wanted to ask Rafael to stay married. For real.

They'd skipped a few steps of the more traditional relationship, but something about that felt right, like it was meant to be. Had they not shown up for each other through this brief relationship—the way a husband and wife would?

The only thing that gave her pause around this entire idea was a simple but important matter—did he feel the same way for her? And after much deliberation and examining the situation from every possible angle Maria came to one conclusion. She needed to tell him how she felt.

Even if sweat appeared on her palms if she just thought of saying those words to Rafael. Though they were true, and her intention was only to let him know her feelings for him, a part of her balked at the thought of betrayal. Daniel had gone back on their implicit agreement as a family. He had put his own needs ahead of everyone else's and almost ruined their legacy by doing so. Was she not doing the same by going back on their agreement that this was a fake relationship and nothing more? Was it wrong to *want* more?

The door behind her opened, and as Rafael walked in with a veiled expression Maria knew the choice had just been taken out of her hands. She needed to tell him, or she would never forgive herself.

He smiled, though something lay beneath it, a reluctance that sent a cold shiver tingling down her spine. There was something amiss. Did he guess what she was about to tell him and that was where the faint displeasure she could see in his face came from?

'What's wrong?' she asked before she could stop herself, wanting to know the answer despite the premonition pooling in her stomach that it wouldn't end well for her—*them*.

'I wanted to apologise for the media circus my family put you through, but it's feeling like this did way more good than it did harm,' he said as he walked over towards her.

He didn't take the empty chair next to her but rather elected to stand, his hip leaning against the desk as he crossed his arms in front of his delectable chest.

'What *were* they trying to achieve?' Maria asked.

The question had been at the back of her mind. She'd read the article and scoffed at a couple of passages where the tabloid tried to claim that Rafael was the disgraced son kicked out of the family after wronging them, and that he was now trying to get his hooks into someone else—her, of all people. They clearly hadn't done their research on her or they would have known that she was as broke as they got. No one ran a charity because they wanted to become rich.

Rafael's expression turned dark as he shook his head. 'This was them sending a message to me.'

'A message?' Maria furrowed her brow, her rise in tone prompting him to elaborate.

'They wanted me to know that they know we are married. It wasn't clumsy or an accident that the person who took these photographs rang the doorbell to ask for me. They wanted me to know that they were watching us,' he said, and the darkness in his eyes was different from anything she had seen in him since he'd arrived in her life—completely upending it.

'I don't understand how planting an ostensibly fake story in a small tabloid helps them get closer to your money,' she said as she tried to piece the information together.

Rafael huffed a humourless laugh. 'These are mind games, Maria. They want us to know that they're watching and waiting—for us to show a weakness. They know the only way I will give them anything is if they can use the people I care about—use them against me.'

Maria frowned, worried about how his reaction was the polar opposite to hers. 'This turned out well for us in the end though, Rafael. Thanks to them, we reached the people we didn't even know mattered.' The obscure intentions of his family were scary, but Maria didn't want to forget about the silver lining to this story. 'Whatever else they have to throw at us, we can take it. Together.'

Rafael's eyes widened when the last sentence slipped through her lips unbidden. Though she hadn't decided on how she planned on initiating this conversation, this starting point seemed as good as any. Because if she didn't say it now, Maria knew that she would never find the courage to say it at all.

'I… I want us to…try,' she began, biting her lower lip when the first words came out in a broken voice. How come she couldn't tap into the confidence she usually felt when it came to talking about her feelings for this man? Especially when she had already shared so much of herself with him. Only one thing remained for her to share with him—that she was his, and that she wanted him to be hers.

'Maria…' Rafael said, but she shook her head as she got to her feet to be on the same level with him.

'I know I'm about to change the agreement

that we had, and I hope you know I'm not doing it lightly. But I need you to know that I'm willing to try being in this relationship for real. Not because at the end of it there is a big donation, but because of you. Because I'm in love with you.'

The sound of her shaky breath was the only sound in the room as they kept staring at each other. Maria grew more and more nervous as the silence went on, her heart squeezing so tight she knew any more pressure would break it. It—along with so much more—now lay in his hands, to do with as he pleased.

He sighed, and when he did it seemed to cut the ground from under her feet, making her stagger back.

'Oh, my God…' she whispered, her wide eyes scanning his pained expression. 'I can't believe I was wrong about this. You…don't love me.'

Rafael stiffened at those words, his hand reaching for her, but she took a step back, evading his grasp. 'No, Maria, that's not—'

'I'm such a fool. I thought there was something between us, something that existed before we even entered into this agreement. This is all my own fault for letting it get so far.' Maria shook her head, biting her lower lip to force the sting in her eyes away. She would *not* let him see her cry.

'Love has nothing to do with this.' He raised his hand, indicating the space between them. 'Don't you see what my family has done the moment they figured out that you mean something to me? They are relentless when it comes to pursuing what they believe to be theirs.'

'So they alerted the tabloids about some non-story. That served us quite well.' Maria took another step backwards, bracing her hands on the table behind her. Her mind was racing, looking for ways out of this conversation she had let herself have with him. How was it possible that he didn't feel the same way? Was everything that happened between them really no more than a figment of her imagination? The night they'd spent together simply to satisfy a physical need that had been building for both of them?

'I told you, that is only the beginning. They won't stop at that and will find ways to insinuate themselves into...' His voice trailed off, and Maria realised it was because he didn't know how to end the sentence. He didn't know what they were, hadn't bothered to think about it.

'You know exactly what I went through with my brother. I can handle myself,' she replied, unsure of what she hoped to achieve. Was she trying to convince him that what they had was worth fighting for?

'But *I* cannot go through the heartbreak again. I can't be the person to bring such chaos into your life. No, I won't. They *will* find a way to get to you as long as we are close,' Rafael said, his face a mask of the ancient pain he'd shared with her in the past few weeks they had spent together.

A tremor took hold of her hands as she dug them into the wooden desk behind her. It took her several breaths to put his words into context and a few more to understand what he was saying.

'Are…you leaving? After everything? Regardless of this marriage, you never said you'd be leaving… Rafael…'

The muscles along his jaw tightened, his hazel eyes that were normally filled with so much kindness and affection suddenly cold as stone.

'That's why I said from the very beginning this can never be more than the deal that we agreed on. I don't *want* to leave, but that was always my plan. I can't stay here, not now that my family knows you mean something to me.'

'What…?' The word came out in a hushed whisper as the scene before her unfolded, none of it making any sense. Because this man in front of her with the ironclad defences surrounding him was not the man she had spent the last four weeks with. He wasn't who she'd fallen in love with.

'So you made the decision to leave all on your own to...protect me, without even asking me first? Why? Because you don't trust me?'

Rafael sighed again, his gaze dropping to the floor. His hands, tightly curled fists at his sides, relaxed before he raised them to his face to scrub over it.

'It's not you, Maria. I don't trust *them*, not after everything that's happened.' He stopped to look at her, and the look of profound sorrow shining in his eyes burst her heart into a thousand tiny pieces.

With a frown he continued. 'I came here to tell you that I'm leaving tonight, and I know eventually you'll understand why I had to do that.'

'Understand?' She crossed her arms in front of her, her jaw clenched so tight the muscle throbbed with pain. 'All this time I thought we were in this together...that you might not love me but at the very least care about me.'

'I do this *because* I care for you, so much more than I could have ever anticipated. They might sniff around here for a while, but once they notice I'm gone they will hopefully leave you alone, since you're not the one controlling the bank account.' He reached down, picking up the backpack and slinging it over his shoulder. 'I really wish it didn't have to end like this.'

Maria swallowed hard, then raised her chin when he made to touch her. 'It doesn't have to, Rafael. If you don't feel the same way for me, just say it and we'll go back to what we agreed on. But I don't need you to decide for me what I'm capable of handling. I thought you knew me better than that.'

His hand stilled in mid-air, as if her words had struck him in a place only he could feel. Something in his eyes softened, showing the wealth of pain he tried to hide despite his masked expression. Then he turned around and left through the door—as if he had never entered her life and completely reshaped it.

CHAPTER TEN

'You're sure about this, *amigo*?' Sebastião asked, looking at him over steepled fingers.

'Yes, I'm sure. It's what we agreed on, so let's get the ball rolling.'

Rafael sat in the all too familiar office of his lawyer in Manaus, trying to tie up the remaining loose ends of his marriage to Maria. *Trying* because every time he thought about ending this wonderful and amazing thing that had grown between them his heart pounded against his chest as if it was determined to escape, his hands getting sweaty, and it became harder to breathe. He'd told Sebastião about that as they'd sat down, needing to get this off his chest.

Sebastião had suggested that he was having a panic attack, though Rafael wasn't ready to admit what that meant regarding his feelings for Maria. She had said what he had been too afraid to admit—facing him with bravery and resolve when he could do no more than walk away. What kind of man wouldn't fall in love with her?

Though being in love with her didn't change that they were doomed to fail. The damage done to him was too severe to be repaired, not even by the loving touch of the most amazing woman he'd ever met.

'Walk me through what happened again? The divorce seems a bit…abrupt,' Sebastião said, and Rafael sighed.

'She told me she loved me and that she wanted to have a relationship with me without the pretence. She wanted us to try to be together.' A searing pain buried itself between his ribs as he recounted the devastating moment, the memories still clinging to him whenever he let his mind wander for too long.

'And why did you say no to that? It sounds like this is what you wanted.' Sebastião cocked his head, eliciting another sigh from Rafael.

'It's not as simple as you make it out to be. My feelings aside, it was never supposed to be real. She needed the money for her charity, and I…' His voice trailed off just as a smirk appeared on the lawyer's face.

Because Rafael didn't know how to complete the sentence. He'd wanted to help his friend, but even that excuse didn't hold up to closer inspection. She and the village had been so warm and welcoming, letting him join the community without a single question, so when the moment to repay her had arisen he couldn't say no—even though he knew it meant the end of his time in Santarém.

'You wanted to help the woman you love,' Sebastião said, finishing the sentence for him and verbalising his thoughts.

'I *can't* love her, Seb. They will find a way to ruin it,' Rafael gritted out between clenched teeth.

'What makes you so sure of that?'

'When I started dating Laura—'

'Let me stop you right there. Laura was an opportunistic socialite who would do anything for exposure and fame. She would fit perfectly with the rest of your family. And you were so much younger back then. So I think you can finally stop beating yourself up for trusting her. If you don't find it in you to forgive yourself, you won't ever get to move on—not truly.'

The jovial twinkle in Sebastião's eyes vanished, replaced by a serious expression as he spoke to Rafael on a level that hardly anyone had spoken to him before. There was a truth in this situation that made him perk up and pay attention to himself the way he hadn't done before.

Forgive himself? Was that the demon that had been plaguing him since the painful incident with Laura and their broken engagement?

He swallowed when a lump appeared in his throat. 'I…just want to keep her safe,' he said, but the words felt wrong on his tongue.

His lawyer must have heard it too, for he shook his head. 'From what you've told me, Maria went through her own share of trouble and managed to remain standing by her own merits. She doesn't need you to deny your feelings to protect her.'

Rafael balled his hands into fists, bunching up the fabric of his trousers. 'Okay, *I'm* the one who is scared. Is that what you wanted to hear? I'm too broken to let anyone near me because the thought of this turning out the same way…'

'You are letting *one* experience ruin the rest of your life. Which brings me back to my point—when are you going to forgive yourself? Because someone like Maria won't be waiting around for you to get your life together.'

Rafael scoffed. 'You say it as if it is the easiest thing in the world.'

'It's not as hard as you pretend it is. What

would happen right now if you went back to her, admitted your feelings and lived as if you were truly married?'

Rafael paused, letting the image take root inside of him. What would happen if he went back to confess his love for her? They would run the charity together, become the family both yearned to have. The money he had been cursed with would go to the noblest purpose he could think of, and he would support his wife as she advocated for the most vulnerable creatures in the rainforest.

And his family? They would be circling like sharks, wanting their bite out of his little slice of paradise that he had built for himself and her. They would try, but Maria was the best person he knew without a shadow of a doubt. When she'd learned she didn't need money from big donors she had been so relieved, glad that she could save the animals with the help of ordinary people.

This woman had said she loved him. Him, who was so wholly unworthy of her affection that he had pushed her away instead of accepting this blessing life had bestowed on him. He had let a mistake he'd made get in the way of what could have been the rest of his life.

'It would be so good,' he whispered after a

few moments of silence, prompting Sebastião to smile at him.

Rafael blinked several times, clearing away the remnants of his daydream as realisation thundered through him. How could he be so arrogant to pretend he knew what was best for Maria when his own fear of loss was driving his decision-making process? There was no way someone like her would ever be influenced but, instead of showing up as bravely as she had, Rafael had let his fear take over and he'd pushed her away.

And with it a life he desperately wanted to live.

He surged from his chair. 'I have to go back,' he said as he looked at his lawyer.

'There we go, you got there.' Sebastião paused to push away from his desk, accessing a drawer. He retrieved a paper folder and put it in front of him.

'The bank has released the funds. They are currently still in the trust's account, so I would advise you to move it to a new bank soon. You still want me to make the donation to Maria's charity?'

The money hadn't even entered his mind. Rafael paused for a moment, then he said, 'Donate the entire sum.'

Sebastião looked at him with raised eyebrows. 'You want me to donate all of your wealth?'

'Yes, donate it all to her charity, and let my family know that what they are looking for is gone for ever. I'm not keeping any of it, I don't need it. Maria does, and so do her animals, so let the people who really need it have all of it.'

Sebastião didn't argue, something Rafael was grateful for as he grabbed his phone out of his pocket, looking at available flights as he prayed that his foolishness hadn't cost him the best thing to ever happen to him.

He stopped when an idea popped into his head. 'Give me two hours to buy something, then send whatever is left over.'

'Is Tia okay?' Mirabel's voice was no more than a whisper, yet it carried far enough for Maria to hear.

'She will be okay, yes,' Celine replied, a lot more audibly, and Maria almost smiled at that. It was very much like Celine to use this moment as a teaching opportunity, showing their niece that she could talk to them about their feelings and that people were sometimes sad.

Though from where Maria was standing, she wasn't sure if she could confidently say that she would be okay ever again. There was a gaping hole in her chest, her heart shattered into pieces and her life so much emptier. Rafael had made good on his promise and left without looking back, and the clinic hadn't been the same since. Not because of the patients or the revenue from having regular vet appointments—she and Celine had been splitting time doing clinic hours until they could find a new vet. No, something fundamental was missing from her life and that was him.

'Mirabel, could you go to your room while I talk to your aunt, please?' she said, and a moment later Celine appeared in the kitchen and sat down on the chair next to her.

'Bad one today?' she asked, and Maria nodded.

'How did you survive when Darius left you like that?'

Her sister had been married for a lot longer than Maria herself, though she'd spent those years estranged from her husband after he'd fled the country—never to be seen again. It had devastated Celine, especially when she'd found out that she was pregnant with Nina. That they would now share the pain of this experience was so surreal to Maria.

'I didn't have a choice,' Celine replied, and nodded towards the sofa where her daughter was fast asleep, wrapped in a cosy blanket.

'I guess that still holds true. There won't be

any less work just because my heart is broken.' Maria tried to smile at her sister, but she raised an eyebrow in question, clearly not convinced.

'Or you could muster up some more strength within you and fight for him.'

'Not this again,' Maria sighed, her eyes dropping down to the glass of wine she held onto a little too tightly. 'He said he didn't love me, so that's the end of it. I can't make someone love me.'

'And I'll tell you again that this is not true. I bet he didn't say that he doesn't love you. I'm sure he said a lot of hurtful things, but that wasn't one of them.' Celine crossed her arms in front of her chest. 'He doesn't strike me as a liar.'

'He's not,' Maria replied, bristling at the idea that someone would call him a liar.

Even though he had been gone for days, the urge to come to his defence was still a reflex that she didn't quite have under control.

It didn't really matter what words he had said, his actions told her all she needed to know about his desire to be with her. He had left, had *planned* on leaving since the moment they'd entered into their fake marriage agreement—something that had become clear to her over the last few days as she'd replayed that scene over and over. He'd always known his family would do something eventually, and that would be the moment he left.

Except Maria was willing to fight for him, defend him against whatever they had planned for him. If she knew anything it was how to deal with a complicated family.

Did Celine have a point and she might have given up too soon? Because if Maria was honest with herself, she had been petrified to say anything to Rafael as he'd left, trying to find excuses that would make it okay not to share her feelings with him.

'Stop it, Cee!' Maria groaned, burying her face in her hands.

Her sister looked at her with a stark line between her brows. 'I didn't say anything.'

'Yeah, but all your arguing is getting in my brain. I *can't* go back to him.'

'Why not?'

Such a simple question that branched out into a hundred different paths. Why did she not stand up and fight when that was what she did best? Because it was hard? Or because there might be rejection waiting at the end of the path?

No, the truth of what rooted her to the spot and made her unable to move lay much darker and far deeper than whatever superficial excuse she could come up with—the fear that he didn't really love her, and that she had invented this affection between them. That she was incapable of understanding when someone was sincere—be it Rafael or her brother. Could she trust her own feelings?

And if she never asked then no one could prove it fake.

'Because...he doesn't love me. Regardless of what he may or may not have said, I know it's true.' The words turned bitter in her mouth, lying on her tongue like thick ash. She knew that wasn't the whole truth, or at least not as clear cut as she wanted Celine to believe. But she'd had enough of this discussion. Rafael was gone and there was nothing left but to move on from the idea of their marriage turning into something real.

Her sister opened her mouth to reply but stopped herself when her phone buzzed on the table. She picked it up, pressing on the screen for a few moments with a confused look spreading over her features.

'What?' Maria asked, leaning over to see her screen, but Celine pulled away at the last second.

She then smiled, a small but wicked grin that Maria knew all too well from their childhood. It was the smirk she had every time she had been right about something. Though they were eight years apart, her sister had absorbed knowledge like a sponge, understanding the subjects that Maria was studying long before Celine herself would learn them in school.

That look never meant well for Maria's pride.

'I'm pretty sure he does love you,' she said, that smile growing wider as she glanced down at her phone again.

'What? Who is messaging you?' Maria demanded and scowled at her sister when she finally turned the screen around so she could see it.

They were looking at the donation goal on their website again. After the viral video of Rafael rescuing the cats from the skip they had updated the goal to aim higher, though she could see that it had already been surpassed again by one big donation of…

'Seventy-four million *real*?' she breathed, the blood rushing to her face as she tried to imagine that large a sum. Who would donate such a fortune…? 'Oh, no…'

Realisation shot through her like a bolt of lightning, kicking her pulse and brain into overdrive. She stared at Celine in complete bewilderment as no coherent thoughts crystallised in her mind. 'This is almost *all* his money. He told me that's how much was in his trust.'

'So tell me one more time that this man doesn't love you.' Her sister crossed her arms. 'A gesture of love can't get any bigger than that.'

Maria stared at the screen. With such funds they could invest in better technology, expand their operations, maybe even hire some more people to help. Why had he done so much more than they had agreed on?

Was that his way of telling her how he felt?

Maria's heart beat against her sternum erratically, pumping hot blood through her veins that made it hard to think. If it was possible that he loved her the way she loved him, then there was a chance for them. If a piece of his heart belonged to her, she could fight for it.

'I have to—' She stopped when Celine threw her car keys at her, already aware of what her sister was saying.

'Get out of here and get him back.'

Slipping into her shoes, Maria reached for the door handle when the video intercom rang. 'You have got to be kidding me…'

She brought up the feed and paused when a familiar face looked back at her. Her breath caught as she hurled the door open and sprinted to the front of the clinic, right into Rafael's out-stretched arms.

She felt the vibrations of his voice as he mumbled something into the thick curtain of her hair, his words getting lost in the beating of her own heart in her ears. Maria pressed herself against him, her arms slung around his midsection as if to anchor him to this spot in front of her clinic—right where he belonged.

'What did you do?' she said when she leaned back for a moment to look at him.

'I came to try. For real,' he said, mirroring the words she'd said to him last week. 'I let my fear get the better of me, I'm sorry for that. The thought of my family bringing their toxicity into our little sliver of paradise scared me to the core, and I didn't know what to do about it. So I found an excuse to keep up my habit of distrust and I ran.'

His expression was grim, his eyes shining with the sincerity that was woven through his apology. Maria shook her head, not needing to hear anything more.

He's back. That was the predominant thought echoing through her head, elevating her heart to new heights as it slowly knit back together.

'I should have fought more. I was scared of

going back on my word and changing our deal when I was the one who caught feelings for—'

Rafael silenced her with a gentle brush of his lips against hers, the kiss vibrating all the way to her bones and drawing out a longing moan. Had it really only been a few days since they'd last kissed?

'You have nothing to apologise for. Now...' He put his hands on her shoulders and gently pushed her away.

Maria gasped when he went down on one knee and presented her with a small ring box with a white-gold band inside. 'I love you, Maria. Have loved you since the moment I met you. I realise we are already married, but I never gave you a ring. So I guess my question is—do you want to turn this into a real marriage?'

Maria nodded, a lump clogging her throat and rendering her unable to answer as tears of joy stung her eyes. Rafael smiled as well, taking her shaking hand into his and pushing the ring onto her finger. It fit perfectly.

'I guess this explains the small part of your fortune that you didn't donate,' she said in jest, as there was no doubt in her mind how expensive this piece of jewellery must have been.

But Rafael only laughed, pulling her back into his embrace. 'The money already arrived?

I'm glad.' He paused, kissing the top of her head. 'I asked Sebastião to transfer everything to you. This money has been lusted after for long enough. It is time it went to something productive.'

Maria smiled into the crook of his neck, breathing in the scent that had been missing from her life for the last week. One that she never wanted to go without.

'I guess that means you need your job back? Because there is no way I'm letting you stay here for free,' she said, joining in as Rafael began laughing.

'I was hoping you hadn't filled that vacancy yet,' he replied.

Maria nodded, cherishing this nearness to her husband—her real husband, finally.

There were many things still to discuss, but those could wait for a few days as they enjoyed their closeness in earnest. They would do this together, that was the only thing that counted. Everything else they would figure out with time.

EPILOGUE

'I REALLY WISH you would let me do this.'

Maria ignored her husband's concerned tone as she put a box down on the exam table, resting one hand on the top of the closed flaps while the other one came to rest on her large belly.

'Rafa, you have stuff going on in the clinic, and I still need to pick up animals whenever they call me, pregnant or not.'

Rafael scowled at her, an expression so full of love that Maria's insides melted. She smiled at him, then grabbed his hand and placed it where hers had just been. 'I know it's your job to worry, but keeping our tiny one safe and sound is my number one priority, okay? I would never do anything that would put us in danger, you know that.'

Ever since their reconciliation, Rafael had got progressively more relaxed when it came to the different dangers his family posed. They had sent a few more private eyes, photographers and lawyers to them to threaten them to release the funds but had eventually given up when they realised that Rafael had given his fortune away to charity.

A charity that he had since taken a larger role in. With the money at hand, they had expanded the building to add more pens and new exam rooms so they could increase their operations. Together they had hired more vets for domestic pets and vet surgeons to help with the injured animals that came in as deforestation efforts in the rainforest increased at a concerning pace.

Rafael had taken on the role of head vet, managing all their newly hired staff and coordinating the daily work that needed to be done—something Maria was eternally grateful for, because it left her plenty of time to look after the animals without having to worry about the clinic.

When she had agreed to marry Rafael out of desperation, she had never dreamed that her charity would look like this. The promised money was supposed to keep them going, but now they had made something to be proud of—and Maria's heart almost burst at the thought that she had done all of this together with her husband, the love of her life.

'Where is Mirabel? I didn't see her back at the house.'

Rafael laughed, the scowl on his face transforming into a bright smile that made her knees wobbly. 'She's cleaning out the pens. When I picked her up from school, she said she wanted to come hang out here.'

'What? She's not spoiling Mamãezinha and her daughters rotten? What have you done to my niece?' Maria shook her head, thinking about the stray cat that had become a new addition to the family—to the great displeasure of Alexander the Great Dane, who now had rivals to his affection.

Her chest expanded with joy and pride she couldn't put into words. Ever since Rafael had taken a more active part in Mirabel's life, her niece had come out of her shell, showing more interest in the world around her and especially in the animals they had in their care.

He had filled a void left by her brother, and Maria would never be able to express how thankful she was. He'd done it without hesitation, embracing Mirabel as his own.

'Speaking of pens… Did I show you the latest pictures of Lia?' she asked.

His eyes widened, his earlier reprimand all but forgotten. When he stepped closer, the familiar scent of lavender drifted towards her and she couldn't help the smile spreading over her face. The moment was one of pure perfection, the like of which she hadn't thought she would ever get to experience.

When he had first arrived in Santarém, Maria hadn't believed that the love of her life had just walked in. Yet here he was, eyes bright and gentle as he swiped through the images to check on the ocelot he had rescued so many months ago. The institute in Manaus sent her regular updates to let her know how their foundling cat was doing.

She added, 'They will try to re-wild her in the next couple of weeks. Maybe if you are up for a little babymoon we could fly down there and wish her farewell. They were able to release the monkeys into the wild already, so chances are we can find them back in Manaus.'

His eyes were still focused on the screen of her phone, and it was clear that her words hadn't found any purchase in his mind.

'She looks so big,' he whispered, and the awe lacing his voice made her chuckle.

Though they worked together a lot more these days, she still forgot sometimes that he wasn't familiar with the kinds of animals she treated every day.

'They grow that large, you know,' she teased

him, and yelped when he shot towards her, hauling her into his arms.

Exactly where she belonged.

* * * * *

*Look out for the next story in the
Amazon River Vets duet*

The Secret She Kept from Dr. Delgado

*And if you enjoyed this story, check
out these other great reads from
Luana DaRosa*

Falling Again for the Brazilian Doc
Her Secret Rio Baby
Falling for Her Off-Limits Boss

All available now!